*Sue Miller*

# Inventing the Abbotts

"These stories report from a frontier, from the discontented and guilty world of divorce and the single parent, of marriage as a threatened institution. . . . The battlefields are the kitchen and the bedroom. Lives are laid bare while the lettuce is washed or another glass of wine is poured. . . ."

—*The New York Times Book Review*

"She has a genius for understanding sexual behavior, and for transforming it into art."

—Hilma Wolitzer

"Sue Miller has the courage and talent to write without tricks. These compassionate and ironic stories are in the mainstream of American fiction."

—Mary Lee Settle

"Reveal[s] the same awareness of modern society that made the author's first novel such a hit. Sue Miller sees the world as a moral stage on which the duties of parenthood must be balanced with the adult need for sexual compatibility—or at least the attempt must be made."

—*Richmond Times-Dispatch*

"*Inventing the Abbotts* more than lives up to the high standard of *The Good Mother*. . . . [The book] shows that she is as deft on a small canvas as she is in the more expansive format of the novel."

—*Seattle Times/Post Intelligencer*

*Also by Sue Miller*

The Good Mother

# Inventing the Abbotts

## and Other Stories

*Sue Miller*

Published by
Dell Publishing
a division of
The Bantam Doubleday Dell Publishing Group, Inc.
1 Dag Hammarskjold Plaza
New York, New York 10017

"Inventing the Abbotts" first appeared in *Mademoiselle* under the title "The Lover of Women."

"Leaving Home," "Tyler and Brina," and "The Quality of Life" first appeared in *The Atlantic*.

"Appropriate Affect" first appeared in *The American Voice*.

"Calling" first appeared in *The Boston Globe Magazine*.

"What Ernest Says," "The Birds and the Bees," and "Expensive Gifts" first appeared in *Ploughshares*.



LAUREL ® TM 674623, Dell Publishing, a division of
The Bantam Doubleday Dell Publishing Group, Inc.

ISBN: 0-440-54070-4

Reprinted by arrangement with Harper & Row, Publishers, Inc.

Printed in the United States of America

Published simultaneously in Canada

June 1988

10 9 8 7 6 5 4 3 2 1

W

*For Maxine Groffsky*

# Contents

# Inventing the Abbotts

Lloyd Abbott wasn't the richest man in our town, but he had, in his daughters, a vehicle for displaying his wealth that some of the richer men didn't have. And, more unusual in our midwestern community, he had the inclination to do so. And so, at least twice a year, passing by the Abbotts' house on the way to school, we boys would see the striped fabric of a tent stretched out over their grand backyard, and we'd know there was going to be another occasion for social anxiety. One of the Abbott girls was having a birthday, or graduating, or coming out, or going away to college. "Or getting her period," I said once to my brother, but he didn't like that. He didn't much like me at that time, either.

By the time we'd return home at the end of the day, the tent would be up and workmen would be moving under the cheerful colors, setting up tables and chairs, arranging big pots of seasonal flowers. The Abbotts' house was on the main street in town, down four or five blocks from where the commercial section began, in an area of wide lawns and overarching elms. Now all those trees have been cut down because of Dutch elm disease and the area has an exposed, befuddled air. But then it was a grand promenade, nothing like our part of town, where the houses huddled close as if for company; and there probably weren't many people in town who didn't pass by the Abbotts' house once a day or so, on their way to the library for a book, or to Woolworth's for a ball of twine, or to the grocery store or the hardware store. And so everyone knew about and would openly discuss the parties, having to confess whether they'd been invited or not.

My brother Jacey usually had been, and for that reason was made particularly miserable on those rare occasions when he wasn't. I was the age of the youngest daughter, Pamela, and so I was later to be added to the usual list. By the time I began to be invited to the events under the big top, I had witnessed enough of the agony which the whimsicality of the list cost my brother to resolve never to let it be that important to me. Often I just didn't go to something I'd been invited to, more than once without bothering to RSVP. And when I did go, I refused to take it seriously. For instance, sometimes I didn't dress as the occasion required. At one of the earliest parties I attended, when I was about thirteen, I inked sideburns on my cheeks, imagining I looked like my hero of the moment—of several years actually—Elvis Presley. When Jacey saw me, he tried to get my mother not to let me go unless I washed my face.

"It'll look worse if I wash it," I said maliciously. "It's India ink. It'll turn gray. It'll look like dirt."

My mother had been reading when we came in to ask her to adjudicate. She kept her finger in the book to mark her place the whole time we talked, and so I knew Jacey didn't have much of a chance. She was just waiting for us to leave.

"What I don't understand, John," my mother said to Jacey—she was the only one who called him by his real name—"is why it should bother you if Doug wants to wear sideburns."

"*Mother,*" Jacey said. He was forever explaining life to her, and she never got it. "This isn't a costume party. No one else is going to be *pretending* to be someone else. He's supposed to just come in a jacket and tie and dance. And he isn't even wearing a tie."

"And that bothers you?" she asked in her gentle, high-pitched voice.

"Of course," he said.

She thought for a moment. "Is it that you're ashamed of him?"

This was hard for Jacey to answer. He knew by my mother's tone that he ought to be above such pettiness. Finally, he said, "It's not that I'm ashamed. I'm just trying to protect him. He's going to be sorry. He looks like such a jerk and he doesn't even know it. He doesn't understand the *implications*."

There was a moment of silence while we all took this in. Then my mother turned to me. She said, "Do you understand, Doug, that you may be the only person at this party in artificial side-burns?"

"Yeah," I answered. Jacey stirred restlessly, desperately. He could see where this was heading.

"Do you understand, honey, that your sideburns don't look real?" Her voice was unwaveringly gentle, kind.

Well, I had thought they might almost look real, and this news from someone as impartial as my mother was hard to take. But the stakes were high. I nodded. "Yeah," I said.

She pressed it. "That they look, really, as though you'd drawn them on?"

I swallowed and shrugged. "Yeah," I said again.

She looked hard at me a moment. Then she turned to Jacey. "Well, darling," she said. "It appears he does understand. So you've really done all you can, and you'd better just go along and try to ignore him." She smiled, as though to try to get him to share a joke. "Just pretend you never saw him before in your life."

Jacey was enraged. I could see he was trembling, but he had boxed himself in with his putative concern for my social welfare. I felt the thrill of knowing I was causing him deep pain.

"Mother," he said, as though the word were a threat. "You

don't understand *anything*." He left the room, slamming the door behind him.

My mother, who never discussed the behavior of one of us with the other, didn't even look at me. She bowed her head in the circle of lamplight and continued to read her book. I left too, after a moment, and was in my room when I heard Jacey hurtling past my door and down the stairs again. His rage had been feeding on itself and he was yelling almost before he got into her presence. "Let me tell you something, Mom. If you let him go to the party like that, I'm not going. Do you hear me? I'm not going." His breathing was audible to me from the top of the stairs—he was near tears—but my mother's answer, which was long, was just a murmur, a gentle flow of her voice for a while. And though he ran out of the house afterward, slamming the front door this time, he was at the party when I got there later. He was dancing and following my mother's advice to pretend he didn't know me.

The reason my entry into his social world, particularly the Abbott part of it, was so painful, so important, to my brother was that he had already fallen in love with their family, with everything they stood for. In an immediate sense, he was in love with the middle Abbott girl, Eleanor. She wasn't the prettiest of the three, but she seemed it. She was outgoing and sarcastic and very popular; and Jacey wasn't the only boy at Bret Harte High trying to close in on her. He spent a long time on the phone each evening talking either to her or about her to girlfriends of hers who seemed to manage her social life through messages they would or wouldn't take for her. He was with her whenever he could be after school and on weekends. But here he was at a disadvantage because he, like me, had a part-time job all through high school, which the other boys in our circle of friends didn't. In this difference between us and the others we knew socially lay, I think, a tremendous portion of the appeal Eleanor Abbott had for my brother.

My father was one of the few in Haley who had died in the Second World War, killed by American bombs actually, while being held prisoner by the Germans. Most of the fathers of our friends had had large enough families by the time America got involved that they didn't go. But my father enlisted when Jacey was two and I was on the way. He died only a few months before my birth, and my mother brought us back to live with her parents in Haley, the small town in Illinois where she'd grown up.

I can't remember my Grandfather Vetter well—he had a heart attack when I was still quite small—but Grandma Vetter was as important as a second parent throughout my childhood. She died when I was ten. We had just sat down to dinner one night when she said, "I think I'll just lie down for a little while," as though that were what everyone did at the beginning of a meal. My mother watched her walk down the hallway to her room on the first floor, and then went directly to the telephone and called the doctor. Grandma Vetter was dead by the time he arrived, stretched out on the bed with her dress neatly covering her bony knees. I remember thinking that there was some link between the way she looked, as though she *were* just resting and would get up any minute, and the way the table looked, every place neatly set, every plate heaped with food, as though we would sit down any minute. I was very hungry, and looking at the table made me want to have my dinner, but I knew I shouldn't care about the food at a time like this—my mother and brother were crying—and I was ashamed of myself.

Throughout my childhood my grandmother preferred Jacey to me—he was a more polite, conscientious boy—and this left my mother and me with a special bond. She was, as I've indicated, incapable of overt favoritism, but she told me later that my infancy provided her with a special physical comfort after my father's death, and I often felt a charge of warmth and protectiveness from her when my grandmother was critical of me, as she often was, in one way or another.

My mother was the only woman in our circle who worked. She taught second grade at the Haley Elementary School, moving to third grade the years Jacey and I would have been her pupils. And, as I've said, we boys worked too, starting in seventh and eighth grade, mowing lawns and delivering papers. By our senior year of high school, each of us had a salaried part-time job, Jacey at the county hospital, I at a drive-in in town. It wasn't that others in our world led lives of great luxury—few besides the Abbott girls did. Our home, the things we did, the kinds of summer trips we took, were much like those of our friends. But my brother and I provided ourselves with many of the things our friends' parents provided them with, eventually even paying most of our own way through college. We were "nice" boys, ambitious boys, but there was a price for our ambition.

Somehow we must have understood too, and yet didn't question, that although our lives were relatively open—we could number among our friends the richest kids, the most popular kids—our mother's mobility in Haley was over. She was single, she needed to work. These facts constituted an insurmountable social barrier for her. Yet it seems to me I barely noticed her solitude, her isolation from the sociable couples who were the parents of my friends. And even if I had noticed it, I wouldn't have believed it could have a connection to the glorious possibilities I assumed for my own life.

Because of our relative poverty, our lives were full of events which were beyond the experience of our friends, but which then seemed only adventurous and exciting to me. For instance, coming back from a car trip to California one summer, we ran out of money. My mother stopped in Las Vegas with a nearly empty gas tank and about three dollars' worth of change in her purse, and won over two hundred dollars—more than enough to get home on—with her second quarter in the slot machine. That kind of thing didn't happen to friends of ours, and somehow, as a result, their mothers seemed more childish to me, less capable, less strong. I thought there was no one else like my mother.

But Jacey yearned for everything she, he, we, were not, and in his senior year of high school, he particularly yearned for Eleanor Abbott.

I'm finally able to see now that at least a part of my passionate embrace of the role of rebel in high school had to do with a need to leap over the embarrassment I could not, out of loyalty to my mother, let myself feel about all those aspects of our lives which I was slowly beginning to perceive as difficult or marginal. I *did* think the Abbott girls and their endless parties ostentatious, ridiculous; but in addition, some private part of me yearned, angrily, for the ease and gracefulness of their kind of life, their sure sense of who they were and how they fit in, as much as Jacey yearned overtly for it.

At the time, though, I thought his yearning, particularly his yearning for Eleanor, was shallow and contemptible. She was a year ahead of me in high school, but even I knew she wasn't smart. In fact, she was in biology with me because she'd flunked it the first time around. I couldn't understand what attracted him to her, especially since I knew she hung around at least as much, and perhaps more—because he was so often busy with his job—with three or four other senior boys.

One summer afternoon, though, the last summer before Jacey went off to college, the drive-in where I worked closed early because the air conditioning was out of order. I came straight home, elated to have an unexpected day off. My mother had gone up to Chicago for a few days to visit a college friend, and I expected Jacey might still be sleeping, since he was working the night shift as an orderly at the county hospital. I was hot, and I felt like celebrating my release from routine, so I charged down the basement stairs two at a time to raid the big freezer. My mother kept it stocked with four or five half gallons of various flavors of ice cream. As I opened the case and leaned into the cool, sweet darkness the freezer seemed to exhale up at me, I heard a rustling noise from the front part of the basement, a whisper. I shut the freezer slowly, my heart thudding, and moved silently toward the doorway. I don't know what I expected—thieves, perhaps—but it wasn't what I saw in the few seconds I stood in the doorway before my brother shouted "No!" and I turned away. He and Eleanor Abbott were naked on the daybed set up near the wall of the coalbin, and Eleanor Abbott was sitting on him. He was in the process of reaching up with his body to cover hers from view when I looked at them. The light in the basement was dim and they were in the far corner—it was like looking at silvery fish in an unlighted aquarium—but the vision lingered with me a long time, clear and indelible.

I left the house immediately—got my bike out of the garage and rode around aimlessly in the heat all afternoon. By the time I came home, it was twilight and my brother was gone. I went down to the basement again. I went into the front room and I lay down on the daybed. I turned my face into its mildew-smelling cover, and imagined that I was breathing in also the rich, mysterious odor of sex.

I remember being less surprised at my brother than I was at Eleanor Abbott. I thought about the three or four other boys she went out with—some of them more seriously than with my brother, I knew from gossip at school. The possibility arose that Eleanor Abbott was having sex, not just normal sex as I'd been able to imagine it with girls I knew, but that she was actually *sitting* on all of the boys she went out with. The possibility arose that Eleanor Abbott, whom I'd seen as utterly vacuous, utterly the conventional rich girl, was a bigger rebel than even I was, in my blue jeans and secret cigarettes, in the haircut I now modeled on James Dean's.

My brother never mentioned what I'd seen, and the silence seemed to increase the distance between us, although I felt a respect for him I'd never entertained before. I saw that even his life could contain mysteries unguessed at by me.

He went away to college that fall on a partial scholarship. I saw Eleanor Abbott around school. Sometimes she'd smile at me in the halls or say hello, especially when she was with friends. I felt that I was somehow comical or amusing to her, and I felt at those moments genuinely exposed, as though what she seemed to think of me was all I really was—a joker, a poser. I discovered, too, that she dominated my fantasy life completely, as she perhaps knew when she'd laugh and throw her head back and say, "Hello, Doug," when we met. Once I actually walked into a door as she passed.

She went to college the next year, to a women's college in the

East. My brother mentioned her several times in letters to my mother, letters she read aloud to me. He said that he'd gone to visit her, or had her to Amherst for the weekend. I don't know what visions this conjured for my mother—she never offered her opinion on any of the Abbotts except to say once that Lloyd Abbott had been "kind of a dud" as a young man—but for me images of absolute debauchery opened up. I could hardly wait to be alone in my room. I found these images nearly impossible, though, to connect with my breathing brother when he came home at Christmas or Easter, ever more trig, ever more polished.

Eleanor didn't come home at the Easter break, I remember, and Jacey seemed to have no trouble finding other women to hang around with. This shocked me, his betrayal of her, in a way that her earlier presumed betrayal of him did not. It seemed, as hers had not, cynical. Hers I had romanticized as wildness, pure appetite.

Sometime in early May I was sitting at the dining room table doing homework, when the phone rang. My mother was in the kitchen, and she called, "I'll get it." She came out to the telephone stand in the hall. Her voice, after the initial hello, was cool and polite, so I assumed it was some social acquaintance of hers and went back to my chemistry. She was silent on the phone a long time, and then she said, sharply and angrily, "No, that's impossible." Her tone made me look up. She had turned her back to me, as though to shield me from whatever was going on. After another, shorter silence, she said, "No, I'm sorry. I can't do that. If you have something to say to my son, you'd better talk to him yourself." I started to stand, my heart thudding, thinking of the various misdeeds of the last weeks, the last months. I ran around at the time with a small gang of misfits, and we specialized in anonymous and, we thought, harmless acts of vandalism—like setting a car upside down on its owner's front lawn, or breaking into the school cafeteria and urinating into the little cartons of orange juice.

"That's right," my mother said stiffly. "I'm very sorry." And she hung up.

After a moment she turned and saw me still standing there, looking, I'm sure, terrified and puzzled. Her worried face relaxed. She laughed. "Sit down, darling," she said. "You look as though you're about to meet your maker."

She came into the dining room and put her hands along the back of the chair opposite me. "That wasn't even about you. It was Joan Abbott, about John." The vertical line between her eyebrows returned. "I'm going to ask you one question, Doug, and if you have no idea, or don't want to answer, just tell me."

I nodded.

She looked down at her hands, as if she was ashamed to be doing what she was about to do. "Is there any sense, do you think, in which John has . . . oh, I don't know, it sounds ridiculous . . . *corrupted* Eleanor Abbott? Led her astray?"

My mind was working in several directions at once, trying to reconstruct the phone call, trying to figure out what the answer to the question might really be, trying to figure out how much I wanted to tell her, and if I told her anything, how to put it.

"Well, I know he's made love to her," I blurted finally. She looked startled only for a second. I could feel a deep flush rise to my face. "But not because he's *talked* about it." She nodded, I think, approvingly. "But . . . I would have said that Eleanor was pretty much in charge of her own life. I mean, she had lots of boyfriends. That she slept with, I think. Even in high school." By now I was talking down to my chemistry book. "I mean, I think he liked her more than she liked him. Not that she didn't like him. I mean, I don't know," I said.

"I see," my mother said. I looked up at her. Suddenly she grinned at me and I felt the pinch of love for her that came only occasionally at this stage of my life. "Well, that was clear as a bell, Doug."

That June, Pamela Abbott, who was in my class, had a tent party to celebrate our graduation. I had been eagerly anticipating seeing Eleanor there, telling her I was going to Harvard in the fall, trying, as I see now, the appeal of my conventional success where the romance of my rebel stance had failed. My brother had been home for a week but he hadn't mentioned her, and some secret, competitive part of me hoped she was done with him, that she would turn to me for the intensity she hadn't found in him.

There was no sign of Eleanor. I danced with her sister once and asked about her; she simply said that Eleanor couldn't make it. But what I heard from others in the course of the evening, in little knotted whispers, was that Eleanor had in some sense broken with her family. Run away somehow. She'd flunked or dropped out of school (something no boy in our world, much less a girl, would ever do), and had taken a job as a waitress or a dancer or an airline stewardess, depending on who told the story.

When I got home that night, I saw the light on in my brother's room. I went and stood awkwardly in his doorway. He was reading in bed, the lower part of his body covered with a sheet, the upper part naked. I remember looking at the filled-in, grown-up shape of his upper body and momentarily hating him.

"Thought I'd report on the Abbott party," I said.

He set his book down. "I've been to the Abbott party," he said, and smiled.

"Well, everyone was there, except you."

"I'm surprised you still go," he said.

"I'm surprised you don't," I said.

"I wasn't asked."

"Oh," I said, with, I hoped, a question in my voice.

"I'm *persona non grata* there," he said flatly.

After a pause, I said, "Eleanor wasn't there, either."

"M-mm," he said. "Well, I'm not surprised."

"I heard she'd left school," I said.

"I heard that too," he answered.

"What's she doing now?" I asked.

"She hasn't told me," he said.

"So you're not in touch with her," I asked.

"No, I've outlived my usefulness to Eleanor." I was surprised to hear the bitterness in his voice.

"How were you *useful* to her?"

"I should imagine that would be easy enough to figure out."

I didn't know what to say.

"I mean," he said, "even aside from the little scene in the basement."

I shook my head, confused and embarrassed.

"Look," he said. "Eleanor was looking for a way not to be an Abbott, to get away from that whole world. And it turns out that it takes a lot to get away. It's not enough that you sleep around with boys from your world. But when you start fucking boys from across the *tracks* . . ." he said. He was agitated. He sat up, throwing back the covers, and got out of bed. He walked to the dresser and lit a cigarette.

"You mean she was sleeping with guys . . . like Prohaska or something?" I tried not to look at his nakedness.

He stood leaning on the dresser. He inhaled sharply on the cigarette and then smiled at me. "No, I mean she was sleeping with me. And she made sure her parents found out about it."

I was silent for a moment, unable to understand. "But *we're* not from across the tracks," I said.

He cocked his head. "No?" he asked. "Well, maybe I'm not talking about literal tracks."

"I don't believe that," I said after a pause. "I don't believe in what you're talking about."

He shrugged. "So don't believe in it," he said. He carried the cigarette and an ashtray back to bed with him, covered himself again.

I persisted. "I mean, we're just the same as them. We're just as good as they are."

He smiled. "Ask the Abbotts about that."

"The Abbotts," I said, with what I hoped was grand contempt in my voice, forgetting for the moment my eagerness to attend Pamela's party.

"Okay. Ask Mom. Ask her about how well *she's* lived in Haley all these years. Ask her whether she's as good as anyone else around here." Then, as though something in my face stopped him, his expression changed. He shrugged. "Maybe I'm all wet," he said. "Maybe you're right." He tapped an ash into the ashtray. "I mean, this is America after all, right?"

I stood in the doorway a minute more. "So what do you think Eleanor is doing?" I finally asked.

"Look, I don't care what she's doing," he said. He picked up his book, and after a few minutes I left.

I went to Harvard in the fall, as did Pamela Abbott—though in those days we still called her part of it Radcliffe. The year after that my brother moved to Cambridge to study architecture at Harvard. Gingerly we began to draw closer together. We still occupied entirely different worlds, mine sloppy and disorganized, his orderly and productive. I thought it emblematic of this that I was so utterly unattracted to the women he preferred. They were neat, wealthy, Waspy and, to me, asexual. I was drawn to ethnic types, women with dark skin, liquid black eyes, wild hair. But I had none. My wild women were abstracts, whereas Jacey had a regular string of real women in and out of his apartment; and I could never look at them, with their tiny pained smiles, without thinking of Eleanor perched on top of my brother in the damp basement the day I wanted ice cream.

We both continued to go home each summer to be with my mother, and it was the summer following his first year in Cambridge, the summer before my junior year, that Jacey fell in love with the oldest Abbott sister, Alice.

Alice had been a year ahead of him in high school, had gone to a two-year college somewhere, and then married. She was arguably the prettiest of the sisters, the most conventional, and if she hadn't been older than he was at a time when that constituted a major barrier, she was probably the one my brother would have been attracted to in the first place. If he had fallen in love with her back in high school, I think their courtship might have proceeded at a pace slow enough, tender enough, so that her parents might ultimately have been reconciled to it; the issue of our marginal social status might have been overcome if it hadn't been combined with Eleanor's sexual precocity; if Alice had come first.

But Alice had married someone else, someone acceptable, and had two children. And now she was back home, something having happened to her marriage. The children were preschoolers; and I was startled once that summer to walk past the Abbotts' house and see a tent set up in the backyard with balloons and streamers floating in the protected air beneath it. I heard children's shouts, someone crying loudly, and I realized that the cycle had begun again for the Abbotts. That if Alice stayed at home, their house, their largesse, would dominate the social world of another generation of Haley children.

I don't know where Jacey met Alice—there certainly were enough people in whose homes they might have bumped into one another—and I can't imagine how he explained himself to her in the context of what her family thought had gone on between him and Eleanor, but he began to see her secretly that summer, arranging to go to the same parties, to meet accidentally. I went out with Pamela every now and then without having any romantic interest in her; we mostly commiserated on how dull Haley was, talked about places around Boston we missed; and she told me about Jacey and Alice.

I said I didn't believe her.

"Alice told me," she said.

"But secretly?" I asked.

"She's afraid of my parents," Pamela said.

"But she's a grown woman, with children. I mean, she's been married, for God's sake."

"Oh, that," Pamela said contemptuously.

"What do you mean, 'Oh, that'?" I asked.

"That was practically an arranged marriage," she said. "They think that Alice has peanut shells for brains or something, so they sort of suggested after she graduated that maybe it was time to tie the old knot, and they sort of suggested that Peter was the one she ought to do it with. Or they just waxed so enthusiastic about him or something that she just did it."

"I don't believe it," I said. I thought of my own mother—how conscientiously she had left Jacey and me free to make our own choices and decisions in life. "No one could be that malleable."

She shrugged. "Look, Alice is the good one, and Eleanor was the bad one, and I'm the one who sort of gets off the hook. I don't know how it got set up that way, but that's the way it works."

We sat in silence for a minute. "What do you hear from Eleanor?" I asked.

She looked at me sternly. "I don't," she said.

I'm not sure that Jacey even slept with Alice that first summer. From what little he said about her, and from what I knew via Pamela, Alice was feeling fragile since the end of her marriage and tentative about getting involved with someone supposedly as dangerous as Jacey. But it was striking to me back in Cambridge that year that he stopped seeing other women. The seemingly endless parade in and out of his apartment stopped; and I was the one, finally, who had women.

I only had two, but it was enough to perplex me thoroughly. I was very involved with theater groups at Harvard; I'd been in one production or another practically nonstop since midway through my freshman year. Now, as a junior, I was getting lead roles; and the exotic women I'd dreamed of having, theatrical women who ringed their eyes with black pencil, were interested in me. But somehow both my romances fell flat, didn't seem as gripping as the roles I played; or even as the tense, delicate relationship Jacey was now maintaining by mail with Alice. Though he wouldn't really talk about Alice with me, about what she was like or what they did together, I knew he was determined to have her, to rescue her the following summer, and I watched it all impatiently.

The summer started and then progressed somewhat as the first one had. There were the frequent phone calls, the arranged meetings. But then Jacey brought Alice to our house.

I suppose they had problems finding places to go together privately, and they finally decided they had no alternative. At first it was when my mother was away, off on her annual trip to a college classmate's in Chicago. I was sitting in the living room, watching television, and I heard them come in. I looked up to see Alice, then Jacey, going upstairs. I could hear the murmur of their voices off and on through the night after I went to bed, and the sounds of their lovemaking, but it didn't bother me as it might have if it had been Eleanor. They left sometime in the dead of the night.

He brought her to the house every night my mother was gone, and we never spoke of it. I don't know what they did in the weeks after my mother's return, but in mid-August, he brought Alice to the house when my mother was home. She didn't hear them come in. She was in the backyard watering the plants; and then for a while I could hear her moving around the kitchen. At about ten o'clock, though, she crossed to the bottom of the stairs and stopped, hearing their voices. Then she came into the dining room, where I was.

"Who's upstairs with John?" she asked.

"I think it's Alice Abbott," I said.

"Oh," she said. "How long is she likely to stay?"

"I don't know," I said. "But I wouldn't stay up and wait for her to leave."

The next morning I didn't have breakfast at home. From the time I woke I could hear Jacey and my mother talking in the kitchen, their voices floating out the open windows in the still summer air, hers steady, kind, and his impassioned, occasionally quite clearly audible. From what he said, I could tell she felt he needed to make his courtship of Alice open. It even seemed she was trying to get him to move out if he wanted to sleep with Alice, perhaps rent a room somewhere. As I left the house, he was saying, "But it's because I do love her, Mother. It couldn't be more different from Eleanor. Eleanor was just an *idea* I had."

I went to the new shopping mall just outside of town and had six honey-dipped doughnuts. I sat next to Evan Lederer—I'd known him in high school—and we talked about summer jobs. Evan was doing construction with a crew working on the interstate, and he had an even, bronze tan to show for it. As we stood together at the cash register, he said, "I hear your brother's taking out Alice Abbott."

"Is that right?" I said.

He grinned and punched my arm.

I don't know what my brother and mother agreed on, but he didn't move out and he didn't, to my knowledge, ever bring Alice to the house again. And then, just before he was to go back to Cambridge and reclaim his apartment from a subletter who was leaving early, it was over. Her parents had found out and simply said no, and apparently Alice didn't have the strength or the financial independence to defy them.

There were several days of phone calls, when my mother and I sat shut in the kitchen or our respective rooms, trying not to listen to Jacey's desperate voice rising and falling, attempting to persuade Alice that it could work if she would just make the break.

And then even the calls stopped, and he just stayed in his room until his job ended and he could leave. And that's literally how he did it. He came home from his last day of work, took a shower, and started loading up his car. My mother tried to persuade him to stay overnight and start the trip the following morning, but he argued that he'd have to drive through at least part of one night anyway, and it might as well be at the beginning of the trip. "Besides," he told her, "the sooner I get out of this fucking town the better."

It shocked me to hear my brother swear in front of my mother, mostly because I took it as an indicator of how deeply lost he was in his own misery; we simply never used that kind of language when she was around. She seemed to put the same construction on it I did, though. Without missing a beat, she said, "Well, of course you feel that way. Would you like me to make you some snacks for the road?"

When he left, she stood looking after his car for a long time. I went up onto the front porch, but she didn't follow. Finally I called to her, "Are you coming in, Mom?" And she turned and began to climb the stairs. I had a sudden revelation then of my mother's age. She had always looked the same age to me—simply *older*—but in that moment she looked as tired as Grandma Vetter had when she told us that she was just going to lie down for a bit.

We had a fairly silent dinner, and afterward, over coffee, she said to me, "Do you think your brother will be all right?"

"Well, he's not going to do anything stupid to himself, if that's what you mean."

"That's not what I mean," she said, her quickly raised hand dismissing even the possibility of that.

"I know," I said. I felt ashamed. Then, impulsively, I said, "I just wish he'd never met the Abbott family."

She sighed. "If John hadn't met the Abbotts, he'd have had to invent them, one way or another. There is no end of Abbotts in the world, if that's what you need. And he just needs that somehow." She picked up the chipped yellow cup and sipped her coffee. "Well, really, I know how."

I was startled. "What do you mean, you know how?"

She sat back in her chair wearily and looked at me. She shook her head slowly. "I think John had a hard time, a terrible time, with the way you both grew up, and it made him want—oh, I don't know. Not money, exactly, but kind of the sense of place, of knowing where you belong, that money can give you. At least in a town like Haley." She shrugged. "And that, the way he grew up, that was my fault."

I answered quickly. "No it wasn't, Mom. If he feels that way, it's his responsibility. I mean, I grew up however he did, and that's not the way I feel."

"Yes, but you're different from John."

I started to protest again, but she lifted her hand to silence me. "No, listen. I can explain it." Then she sighed again, as if coming around to some central, hard truth. "You know that after Charlie—your father's—death, I was just . . . I was just a mess. I hurt so badly that some mornings I'd be crying before I even woke up. And then I had you." She looked up at me. "And poor old John, well, he just got lost in there. I just didn't have anything left for him."

She shook her head. "He was such a sad sack kind of kid

anyway. He'd always been jumpy and intense, even as a baby. I just couldn't settle in and be loving to him. He was too nervous. Whereas *you* . . ." She smiled at me. "You just slept and smiled and nursed. When you were a toddler, I had to pin a sign on the back of your shirt saying, 'Don't feed this child,' because you'd go around the neighborhood and everyone would just give you things.

"And I swear, as I remember it, I spent weeks just sleeping with you in bed after you were born. I got dressed for meals, but that was about it. Otherwise I'd sleep and sleep and sort of come alive just to nurse you or change you. I just couldn't believe Charlie wasn't coming back. I was twenty-four years old." Her face was blank, remembering things I couldn't understand.

She cleared her throat. "And John just floated away from me. My mother was right there, you know, and terribly concerned about me, and she sort of took him over. That was what she felt she could do for me. I can remember early on sometimes I'd hear him crying or calling for me, and then I'd hear her, and after a while he'd stop, and I'd be *glad*. I'd just hold you and go back to sleep. Or more like a trance, it really was. I'll never forgive myself."

I wanted to comfort her. "But he loved Grandma Vetter," I said. "I mean, he ended up getting a lot out of that."

"Well, yes, I think he did, but in the meantime, making that shift from me to her was terrible for him. And I'm not so sure having my mother as a substitute was so good for him. I mean, she was born in another century. All her values and rules, while they're perfectly good ones, were ones that sort of . . . stiffened John, fed *that* side of who he was. And I, I knew that he, much more than you, needed to learn to relax, to be playful. But I just didn't, couldn't, help him." She twirled her cup slowly in its saucer. "And then I was working and he was so good and reliable, and you were the one always in scrapes."

I felt a pang of something like guilt. "But he turned out fine, Mom. He turned out great."

"Oh, I know he did, darling, but I'm talking about something else. I'm talking about why John struggles so hard to have certain things in his life. Or even certain people."

I frowned at her, not sure I understood.

"I let him go, Doug, don't you see?"

I shook my head, resolute on her behalf.

She looked at me for a moment. Then suddenly she said, "All right, I know. I'll tell you. It's like the time, I remember, I was driving you boys back from somewhere . . . Oh, I know where it was. It was that time—I'm sure you don't remember, you were so little—but we'd been out East to visit your dad's folks, and we were coming home through Sandusky. We were going to stop at my great-aunt's for the night. Viola. She's dead a long time now. And I just couldn't find it. I tried for about an hour and a half, but nothing was where it was supposed to be by my directions. And so I finally just pulled over—I was so aggravated—and I said out loud, 'Well, that's it. We're lost.' And I was so busy looking at these directions and maps and things that I didn't notice John for a few minutes. But when I finally looked at him . . . Well, I've never seen a child so terrified. I asked him what the matter was and he said, 'You said we were *lost!*' And suddenly, by the way he said it, I knew he thought I'd meant lost in a sort of fairy-tale sense—like Hansel and Gretel, or someone being lost for years in a forest. Never getting home. Starving to death. I remember feeling just terrible that he had so little faith in me. In my ability to protect him."

She shook her head and smiled ruefully. "You know, most kids his age—he was five or six, I think—don't think they're lost as long as they've got their mother with them. But I knew right then that I'd lost John. Just lost him." She shook her head again.

After a moment I said softly, "I think he'll be all right, Mom."

"Oh, I know he'll be all right, honey," she cried. "I know it! That's what breaks my heart." And for the first time in my memory since Grandma's death, I saw my mother cry.

I went over to Jacey's apartment more frequently that fall than I had in the past. I had a sense of him as a trust that my mother had placed in me. I'm not sure what made for the conviction that she had never spoken about me to him as she'd spoken about him to me; but I felt secure in it. And I felt she'd somehow asked me to help her pay a debt to Jacey that she, and therefore perhaps I too, owed him.

It didn't make much difference to our relationship, because Jacey simply wouldn't speak to me about anything intimate; but in fact, I liked the order and the quiet in his carefully furnished apartment. On Sundays, I almost always bought English muffins and the *Times* and walked over there. We'd sit quietly all morning, eating and going through the paper, occasionally reading aloud or commenting on some story.

But as the fall wore on, I found more and more, when I dropped over unexpectedly, that he'd come to the door in a bathrobe or towel and tell me that it wasn't a good time. He never smiled or suggested in any of the ways some of my friends might have that it was because there was a woman inside, but I knew that's what it was, and I was happy for him; though a little surprised after the intensity of his feeling for Alice. But it was clear to me, by now, that Jacey was a lover of women, that he needed and enjoyed their company in a way that some men don't—perhaps, I remember speculating then, because of my mother's painful turning away from him when he was a young child. That he was again able to be interested in women seemed to me a sign of health, and I wrote my mother that Jacey was, as I put it, "beginning to go out a bit," though he hadn't actually spoken to me about it.

He invited me to early dinner one Friday in late October. Early, because he was doing something later on. It was a cold, rainy night, and I remember a sense of nostalgia swept over me as I walked the short distance to his apartment, stumbling occasionally over the bumps in the rain-slicked brick sidewalks. I was in the throes of another dying romance, powerfully disappointed because the woman I thought I had loved was so much more mundane than I had originally conceived of her as being. Jacey had made a fine meal—scallops and salad and a very good wine.

We had several cups of coffee afterward, and I remember thinking how thoroughly in charge he was of his own life, wondering how many years it would take before I would be able to know what shape I wanted to give my life, let alone do anything about it. He went into his study to get some slides he wanted to show me, and the doorbell rang.

"Shall I get it?" I asked.

"Sure," he called back.

A woman stood under the porch light, wearing a poncho, her head bent down, her face lost in the shadow of her hood. As I opened the glass door, she raised her head. It was Pamela Abbott. She looked startled, but her voice was smooth. "Hello, Doug," she said.

I said hello. For a few confused moments, I thought that she'd somehow come to my brother's apartment to see me; but as I followed her in, I realized this couldn't be, that it was, of course, John she had come for. Even then I couldn't make my mind work to understand it reasonably.

Jacey greeted her coolly and took her coat, shaking it away from him several times before he hung it up. She sat down at the table, and I joined her. He was standing. He asked her if she wanted some coffee. She shrugged. "Sure, if you're having some."

While he was in the kitchen, I felt compelled to make talk. "So, Pamela," I said. "What's up?"

She shrugged again.

"I mean, God," I said, feeling more and more like an idiot, "I'm really sweating out this *facing life* business. Trying to decide what in hell I'm going to do next year, you know?" She looked steadily at me and didn't respond. "Do you have any idea what you're going to do?"

"I don't know," she said. "I'll probably go to New York and get a job in publishing, I think."

"God, that sounds exciting. But it's rough, isn't it? I mean, to get a job?"

"I don't know. My father has a couple of connections. I don't think it'll be too hard to get some shit lower-level thing."

Jacey was standing in the doorway now, a cup of coffee in his hand. "And then climb the ladder, using his connections all the way," he said sharply. I looked at him, but his face was blank. He walked over to her and set the coffee in front of her. She shrugged again. She looked at him as he went back to his seat. I watched her watching my brother, and saw that she was frightened of him. I realized that I should have left as soon as she arrived, that she was what my brother was "doing" later. We sat in silence for a minute. Jacey lit a cigarette and the smell of sulfur and burning tobacco hung in the little room.

"Well," he said suddenly to Pamela. His voice was still sharp. "Do you want to go to bed?"

She looked quickly at me and then away. After a moment she raised her shoulders. "Sure," she said without emotion, as though accepting some punishment. He stood up. She stood up. I stood up. I was trying to meet my brother's eye, and it seemed to me that for a second I did; but his gaze slid quickly sideways. He walked out of the room first, and she followed him, without looking at me again.

I left the apartment immediately. My heart was pounding in my ears. I walked down to the black river in the rain, across the Western Avenue bridge and all the way up to the boathouse on the other side, trying to understand what my brother was doing to himself, to Pamela, to me. He who was so private, who kept his life and emotions so masked, had exposed himself and Pamela to me, had shown me how contemptuously he could treat her, how despicable he could be. He who had felt used, I know, by Eleanor; and who, I could guess, had felt abused by Alice, was now doing both to Pamela. It seemed to me like a violation of everything I would have said he believed in. And I felt slapped that he had asked me to witness it all, as though he were exposing also my pretensions to understand anything about life.

I was cold and drenched by the time I got home. I took a long shower, grateful that both of my roommates were out, and went to bed early. I lay awake for a long time, thinking about Jacey, about myself, about how we had grown up.

I didn't get in touch with my brother or go to his apartment again for several weeks. Finally he called. It was a Sunday. He said he'd gotten the *Times* and made breakfast and he wondered if I wanted to come over. I said okay, not enthusiastically; and then I said, "Will there be just the two of us?"

"Yes," he said. "That won't happen again."

It was cold outside, gray. The trees were nearly stripped of leaves and I had the sense of winter coming on. John had a fire going in his fireplace and had set breakfast out on the coffee table. I was, for once, repelled by the orderliness. I wondered if I'd ever see my brother in a spontaneous moment. I swallowed some of his good coffee.

"I wanted to apologize," he said.

"Oh," I said.

"What I did was wrong."

"Did you tell that to Pamela?" I asked.

"What business is that of yours?" he said, flaring suddenly.

Then he looked away, into the fire for a moment. We were sitting side by side on the couch. "Yes," he said tiredly. "You're right. And I did say it to her. I'm not seeing her anymore. I wanted you to know that." Then he slouched lower in the couch and started to talk. He told me that Pamela had come over unexpectedly almost as soon as school started. It upset him to see her and he had a lot to drink while she was there, as she did. He said she did most of the talking, about her family, about Alice, about Eleanor. She seemed eager to align herself with him against her parents. She told him that they were stupid, rigid. Worse, they were cruel. She said that they had destroyed Eleanor and were destroying Alice; that she was the only daughter smart enough to see the process, the pitfalls on the one hand of resisting too hard, or, on the other hand, of caving in. She called her father a tyrant, a bastard. She said that Jacey couldn't imagine the kinds of things said about him, about our family, in their house.

And then, drunk, she said how wonderful she'd always thought he was; how much she admired him; how much she wanted him. She thought they ought to sleep together.

Drunk too, and angry, he had done it. Then he had passed out, and in the morning she was gone. He said he had thought that that was probably it, that she'd seen herself as fulfilling some part of what he called her "Abbott destiny" by having him as a lover.

But she kept coming over, and he kept sleeping with her. He said he knew it was wrong, that he didn't even like her really. But that in some ways it was like having Alice again, and it was like getting back at her too. And so he just kept doing it.

He got up and poked the fire. He sat down again, this time on the floor. "And then I began to feel *used* again," he said. "It was crazy; I was using her too. But I began to feel that somehow I was just . . . some bit actor in some part of their family drama. She kept telling me she loved me; and I just kept getting more and more cruel to her. More angry." He looked at me suddenly. "I guess inviting you over was a way of seeing how much she'd take, how low she'd go." He turned away again. "I was pretty far gone too, in some kind of rage I'd lost control over. But finally I just said I wouldn't see her anymore. I was trying to be kind, but it ended up being a pretty ugly scene. Lots of tears and yelling."

I thought of Pamela, so flip, so sure of herself. "Did she not want to stop?"

He shrugged. "She claims she's in love with me. She threatened to tell Alice we were lovers if I wouldn't see her anymore."

"God!" I said. "Think she will?"

He shook his head. "I don't know. She may. I'm hoping it'll seem so uselessly cruel that she'll decide not to. But it's her family. And I took that risk when I slept with her. And there won't be anything more between me and Alice anyway, so maybe it'd be for the best. Maybe it'd confirm all the terrible things her father has to say about me, and make things easier for Alice."

"That's pretty magnanimous of you," I said.

He looked at me and smiled. "Not entirely. I'd like to be able to let go of her. It's been hard. I mean, I've been in love with her for a year and a half and I've slept with her maybe ten times. And I never will again. She still writes to me all the time, even though I can't answer. That kind of stuff. I mean, maybe it's part of the whole thing. Why I slept with Pamela in the first place. To push that possibility away forever."

We talked on into the late afternoon, sometimes about other things—his work, my theatrical ambitions—but we'd always circle back to Alice and Pamela. When it began to get dusky, Jacey got up and turned the lights on. I stretched. I told him I had to go. I took the theater section of the *Times* and headed back to Adams House.

That was the end of my brother's involvement with the Abbott girls. He told me a few Sundays later that he thought Pamela must have said something to Alice or to her family, because the letters abruptly stopped, but otherwise we didn't speak of them again. I went home the following summer and he stayed in Cambridge. He had a drafting job with a little design company. Alice was still living at home and I saw her a few times during the summer. At first I didn't recognize her. She'd put on at least twenty-five pounds. She didn't say hello to me, but I didn't really expect her to. In fact, as if by some unspoken agreement, we each pretended not to know the other when our paths crossed.

In the fall I moved to New York. I saw Pamela there occasionally, for a few years. We still had friends from college in common. She was an assistant editor at a good publishing house, and I was trying to get any kind of acting job. We'd talk when we met, a little edgily. She'd ask about Jacey, and I'd ask about Alice and Eleanor, as if they were vague acquaintances, and not a part of who we both were. She was in touch with Eleanor again, but Eleanor refused to see the family at all. She was a stewardess, and she loved it, loved to travel, Pamela said. Alice lived at home and let her parents run her children, her life. Pamela went home every now and then for a few days, which was about as long as she could stand it, she said.

Our only really difficult conversation was our last one, when I had to tell her that Jacey had gotten married. She looked pained for the smallest fraction of a second, and then the tough smile reemerged. "Well, I assume that whoever it is is rich."

"Why do you assume that?" I asked. In fact, Jacey's wife, an architect too, did have some money, perhaps even as much as the Abbotts had. But I knew enough now to know that that really wasn't rich. And Jacey seemed happy no matter what.

"Isn't that the only kind of girl he's ever been interested in?" she asked jauntily. "Hasn't he been trying to marry *up* since about the day he had his first erection?"

There were so many levels on which her remark offended me—the insult about Jacey's intentions, the implied insult about his, and therefore my, social class—that I wasn't able to choose at which level I wanted to respond. I answered quickly, almost without thinking, "Why do you assume that for him to have married one of you would be to marry up?"

She looked at me for a moment with her mouth open, and then she turned away.

I didn't see her again before I moved to Chicago. I wanted to be nearer my mother, who wasn't well, and I'd gotten a good job with a repertory company there.

My mother got worse over the next three years—she had cancer—and I often went down and spent two or three weeks in the old house with her when there were breaks in my work. One summer night we were driving past the Abbotts' and the tent was up again. Dance music swelled out on the summer air. The band was playing "Blowin' in the Wind" to a bouncy fox-trot rhythm. My mother looked over at the soft yellow lights, the moving figures. "Imagine a child of Alice's being old enough to dance," she said. And I recalled, abruptly, that she had known all the Abbotts, all the children in town, really, as second graders. That in some sense we remained always young, always vulnerable in her vision. She didn't think of the pain we'd all caused each other.

She died in the early winter of that year. I went down frequently in the fall. We sat around at home in the evenings, often drinking a fair amount. She'd lost so much weight by then that she was, as she called herself, a cheap drunk; and we seemed to float back easily into the comfortable, desultory intimacy we'd had when I was home alone with her in high school. Once she asked me what came next for me in life. I asked her what she meant. "Oh, I don't know, darling," she said. "You just seem so content, I wonder if this is really . . . *it* for you."

"I don't know," I said honestly. I felt, at the moment, so peaceful that it wouldn't have bothered me if it was. "It seems to me I've chosen the right profession, certainly. I'm really much better at pretending than at being. You know, I used to have such contempt for Jacey, for what he wanted out of life, for the kinds of women he went after. But in fact he always really went after things. And he suffered with it, but he's all right in the end. I like him. Whereas I haven't done that. I'm happy, but . . . Well, that's all that really counts, I guess. I am happy. I'm actually very happy."

"I know what you mean," she said. "I've been happy too, and glad I didn't have the messes that some of my friends made of their lives. But sometimes I've worried that I lived a little like a nun, you know. Sort of a *pinched* life, in the end."

We sat. The only sound was the occasional faint noise of the old house shifting somewhere slightly in the cold fall air.

Then I said, "Why didn't you ever remarry, Mother? Surely there were possibilities."

"Fewer than you'd think," she said. "Everyone always thinks things are more possible than they are. I mean, single men don't stay in Haley if they've got any starch. Who was there my age who was eligible? Drew Carter was always around, but he's a washout. And now there's a few old widowers who smell like their dogs." She laughed. "I'm getting mean," she said. "And then I was a schoolteacher for all those years. You don't meet men in a job like that. No, the only time I ever met anyone was in Chicago, a friend of Beatrice Goulding's. I used to go up and visit him every summer, stay with him for five or six days. Surely you remember that. I always told you I was staying with Beatrice." I nodded. I remembered those visits. "He was a wonderful man. Wonderful." And then, with that deft way my mother had of casting the entire story she was telling in a new light, she said, "A little boring, but really, very wonderful."

"Well, why didn't you marry him? Move us all up there?"

"Oh, I couldn't have done that to John," she said instantly. "He'd had such a terrible early childhood, and he was so happy at that stage. Remember? He was playing ball and had a good job and was chasing around after that middle Abbott girl. No." She shook her head. "All this life in Haley had gotten to be too important to him then. I can't imagine having asked him to give it up. I never would have forgiven myself. No, it was better for me to go on as I had been. And besides, I was still really in love with Charlie. With my memory of him. And I've enjoyed my life. I have," she said wistfully.

"Well, it's not over yet," I said.

But it nearly was. Jacey came out for the eight or ten days before she died. We took care of her at home, as she'd wanted, with a visiting nurse to help us. She was very uncomfortable the last few days, though not in actual pain, and I think we were both relieved when her struggle stopped, when we didn't have to listen to her trying to breathe anymore in the night.

There wasn't really a funeral, because she'd been cremated and because she didn't want a service. She had requested that we have a hymn sing, and she had written down three or four of her own favorites she wanted us to be sure to do. Jacey and I discussed the plans the morning after she'd died. We were washing the last of her dishes, putting things away in the kitchen. "Isn't it like her," he said, tears sitting in his eyes, "to want to control even the way we let her go." He shook his head in proud amazement, and I thought how differently we knew her, understood her.

So we gathered, around twenty or so of her friends, mostly women, and Jacey and I, and some young people who were former students; and sang "Guide Me, O Thou Great Jehovah" and "Fight the Good Fight" and "Amazing Grace" and "For All the Saints." It seemed so insufficient, as any service does, I suppose, that we went on singing too long to compensate, and Jacey and I were both hoarse the next day.

But there were still things to pack up, and so we went to the old center of town to get some boxes. It was a cold, bright day, and the town looked small and shabby in the raw light, as though nothing important could ever have happened there. We were loading the trunk and the back seat of the car in front of the liquor store, when I saw a woman walking toward us down the street whom I recognized instantly as Mrs. Abbott. She didn't look very different from the way she had at all those parties. Her hair, dyed now, I suppose, was still a pale arranged blond; her lipstick was a girlish pink. She saw Jacey, and I could tell that for a moment she was thinking of walking past us without acknowledging us; her step wavered marginally. But then she made some internal decision and approached. Jacey saw her and straightened up. We both assumed, I think, that she would speak to us of our mother's death, which is what every conversation we'd had in the last few days had started with.

But whether she didn't know what we were both in town for, or whether her own emotions of the moment drove it out of her mind, that's not what she spoke of. A brilliant social smile flickered quickly across her face and was gone. Then, standing an uncomfortable distance from us on the sidewalk, she made for a minute or two the kind of small talk she'd made all those years ago under the tents in her backyard—a comment on the weather, on how we'd changed, on how busy young people's lives were, they could hardly ever get home anymore. As she spoke she nodded repeatedly, an odd birdlike motion of her head. There was an awkward silence when she finished—I know I couldn't imagine what an appropriate response would be—and then she said with brittle cheer to Jacey alone, "Well, I've no more daughters for you." And as though she'd been talking about his loss rather than her own, she smiled again, and walked on.

For a moment we stood motionless on the sidewalk, watching her diminishing figure. Then I turned to Jacey, expecting, I suppose, some comment, and ready to be angry along with him, on his behalf. Instead he bent down and started again to load the empty boxes that would hold my mother's belongings into the car, as though what Mrs. Abbott had just said and done had all happened years before, with the rest of it, when he was a child.

# Tyler and Brina

Tyler loved women. He was in love with women. He saw them in shops, on the subway, at work, and imagined them falling back over and over, laughing, crying, soft, wet. He had a hard-on half the day. He didn't much care what they looked like. The firm girls with T-shirts ending above their navels who weighed his fruit at the grocery store. His secretary, with the little rim of fat riding over her girdle and her sad eyes. He stood, offering a plum, holding out a bill, and he loved them. He wanted to lift the hair out of their eyes, to slide his hand down over the tops of their blue jeans onto their tanned bellies, to push them down—so gently!—to make them smile, open their mouths, to make them cry out softly, to take their pain away.

He had thought this might change when he married Brina. He had hoped it would. But even though he slept around less, he still yearned after women all the time, yearned for their gentleness, their loving response, their sweet dampness.

Now Brina wanted a divorce. She'd moved out and was living in an apartment belonging to a woman from her office who was on vacation. Tyler dropped by nearly every evening after Petey was asleep. He wanted Brina back. He made love to her again and again on the living room couch where she slept at night, often with all his clothes on, Brina's skirt wrinkled into a thick belt at her waist. Something about seeing her like that in the purplish light of the streetlamp which flooded into the room drove him on. Even when he couldn't come anymore, he was hard, he wanted her. "Oh, you asshole," she'd moan. "You motherfucker. God, I hate you. I hate you."

Petey was seven years old. He was Brina's son by her first marriage. She wouldn't let Tyler see him anymore. She thought it would be difficult for Petey. It had been difficult for him to get used to Tyler in the first place. It had taken nearly the whole year he and Brina had been married. As recently as a few months before Brina moved out, Petey would take the opportunity, if he and Tyler were wrestling or tickling, to punch or kick Tyler as hard as he could in the groin. Once Tyler had heard Petey actually whisper to himself, "Get him!" before he struck.

The morning of the day that Brina left him, Tyler had taken a shower with Petey. He had squatted down under the spray and let Petey scrub his back. Petey's wiry small body felt strange gliding across Tyler's back and buttocks while Petey scrubbed. Then Tyler felt a short stream of lukewarm water on his back, and Petey said, "I spit on you, Tyler, did you feel it? I spitted right on you." Tyler turned, still squatting, to look at Petey. He was grinning expectantly with his mouth open, the water flattening his blond hair dark against his small, neat head. Tyler felt the sense of uneasiness he often felt with Petey and never felt with women, a sense of not knowing what the next move ought to be.

"Now can I get you?" Tyler asked.

"Yeah!" Petey said. His body jigged in anticipation.

Tyler tipped his head up into the spray and filled his mouth. He squirted the water onto Petey's chest. Petey laughed, and

Tyler laughed with him, partly in relief that he'd chosen the right thing to do.

"I can't even feel it," Petey said. "I can't even feel it because I'm *already* wet."

Tyler had seen Brina smile at them through the clear plastic shower curtain while she put her makeup on. He had felt a sense, suddenly, of the three of them as a family, locked together irrevocably. Something about this rekindled his feelings of uneasiness, and he stood up and turned away from Petey to rinse himself off. But when they had dropped Tyler off at the subway on the way to Petey's school, her work, he had kissed Brina's mouth, had rested his hand briefly on Petey's damp hair.

Tyler was a contractor and a part-time developer. He owned and managed eight small apartment buildings around the city. He'd bought them one by one, including the one he and Brina lived in, and done the renovations on them himself. That night just before he left the office, one of his tenants called. Someone had broken into her apartment, had stolen her television set and stereo. The lock on her door had been broken, and the super was out for the evening—he'd left a note by his buzzer. She was afraid to stay overnight by herself unless someone fixed it. Tyler called Brina and told her he'd be late for supper, not to wait. He took the truck and stopped at the hardware store for a new lock, and a chain because he guessed that the extra protection would reassure his tenant.

When he arrived at her apartment, she was sitting in the entryway with the door swung open, smoking a cigarette and drinking what looked like whiskey. "Oh, thank God you're here," she said. She stood and stubbed out the cigarette. "Look, just look at what these jerks did to my house!" She gestured behind her toward the living room. Tyler could see records in and out of their jackets spilled all over the floor. Papers were strewn everywhere.

"And look in here," she said. She walked down the hall ahead of him. She was wearing heels and a skirt. Tyler watched her legs, the quick shifting gleam of the light on her stockings as she moved in front of him. She stood in her bedroom doorway. It was worse in here. Her clothes had been dumped from the drawers. The closet yawned open, the empty hangers angled awkwardly this way and that. "It just makes me feel so *violated,*" she said.

Tyler had heard it before. Several of his buildings weren't in such great neighborhoods. He was carefully sympathetic, though. He talked to her for a while before he started working on the door. When he'd finished, she offered him a beer and asked him to sit down for a few minutes before he left, just until she calmed down. She had been working in her bedroom, and she'd changed into jeans and a fuzzy pink sweater. Tyler sat on the couch, and she curled up in a large chair opposite him. They talked about insurance, what kinds of coverage they had. Then he asked her about her work. She was a social worker, she said. She worked with juvenile offenders. "In fact," she said, and giggled, "the chances are excellent that some *client* of mine pulled this little number tonight."

Tyler smiled and gently shook his beer can. Almost empty.

"Oh, I'm going to miss my record player," she said abruptly. "I was just thinking how usually when people are over I play music while we talk. Course, I've got a radio. Do you want some music?" She was a little drunk, too serious. Tyler grinned and shrugged. "I'm going to get my radio," she said. "You stay right there." She got up and ran down the hall. When she returned, Tyler noticed she wasn't wearing a bra under the sweater. She looked up from plugging the radio in and caught him staring at her. As she sat down next to him on the couch, they were both smiling as if they already shared some kind of secret.

When he called Brina at her job, about ten the next morning, she said, "Oh, God, you're all right." There was a long silence, and then she said more softly, "I called the hospitals, but you weren't there." He could hear that she was starting to cry.

"No," he said. And then, "I'm sorry."

After a minute, she said in a pinched voice, "How can this be? I don't want this to happen, Tyler."

"I'm sorry," he said.

"But *what?* What do you plan?" she said. "How can this be?" She was crying openly now. He could imagine her in her office, trying to cover her face in case anyone walked in.

"Can we talk about it tonight? Can I come home?" he asked.

"Home?" Her voice soared to an unfamiliar, awkward register on the word. "Home?" she asked, and then she hung up.

One side of Brina's face was dead, injured in a childhood accident. When they made love, Tyler, for some reason, lay more often with his head on that side of hers. Looking at her, he was sometimes startled by the stillness on her face, as though she were in a deep dreamless sleep. "Oh oh, oh God," she would cry in an agonized voice from her blank face as Tyler lowered his head to her shoulder, his body hard at work. When she smiled, half of Brina's face lit up, and the rest lifted only slightly in sympathy, as though, Tyler thought, she knew of some deep sorrow that lay under every fleeting joy.

When Tyler first saw her after he'd slept with Meredith, the live side of her face was distorted with rage, and both eyes were puffy from sleeplessness and tears. He'd gone home first, but she wasn't there. Their apartment looked a little like Meredith's the night before. Brina had pulled things out of drawers and left them all over their bedroom, Petey's bedroom. The suitcases that usually sat on the top shelves of their closet were gone. Tyler felt such a sense of desolation that for a moment he thought of leaving the apartment too, of going somewhere to have a drink. But he didn't. He got out their Rolodex and began to call their friends, Brina's friends, until he found someone who knew where she had gone. In a cold voice, Marietta said, "Well, I suppose you'll find out anyway," and gave him the address.

It was about ten o'clock when Tyler got there. The building was an old triple decker in a run-down part of town where mostly students and blacks lived. Under the stairs in the entrance hall were baby carriages, someone's cross-country skis, heaped-up boots. From the first-floor apartment came laughter and Otis Redding. Tyler mounted the stairs. On the second floor, the name he was looking for, Eliopoulos, was printed on masking tape above the doorbell. He rang and waited. Then he rang again. He could hear Brina blowing her nose. The door opened. She looked at him for a moment, half of her face pulling into hard, angry lines. Tyler tried to look at the other side, her sad eye, her drooping lips. Abruptly she stepped forward and began to hit him. She hit him sharply with her fists, four times, then stepped back and slammed the door. Neither of them had said anything, though Brina had made a little noise of effort with each blow. She had been swinging awkwardly, from the side, and Tyler covered his head as well as he could after the first blow smashed into the side of his nose, but one of his ears was ringing dully as he left, and when he reached up to touch it, his hand came away wet with blood.

He had stopped in a drugstore on the way home to get disinfectant and a styptic pencil. He stood in front of a display of panty hose thinking about Brina, about what he could do to get her to talk to him. He knew if he could just talk to her, just get his hands on her—he could see his hands slide across the top of her bathrobe onto her breasts—things would be all right. She was all he wanted.

"Can I help you find something?" the girl asked. Tyler looked at her. Freckles, long straight hair. She was wearing a pale blue drugstore smock and very tight jeans. She smelled of Juicy Fruit chewing gum. She smiled at him. A big gap between her two front teeth touched Tyler's heart, and he smiled back. "Yes," he said.

Tyler was careful with Brina. He didn't bring flowers or presents; he didn't call or try to get in touch with Petey. He just kept coming over. At some point, he knew, she would have to take responsibility for his silent presence outside her door. It took a week and a half for her to let him in, and twenty minutes after that, Tyler was making love to her on the couch. He pushed up onto his elbows to look at her. She had her face turned away from him, and her eyes were shut. She seemed trusting, utterly at peace. Tyler's heart welled with remorse and gratitude toward her and he began to weep softly. She turned to him, and he saw that her face was remote, cold, full of a hard anger. "Brina," he said, frightened. He couldn't believe she could make love with him without feeling love. He touched her face gently, as though he could change what he saw with a gesture.

"Don't talk to me," she whispered furiously, and pulled him to her.

Now Tyler began to woo Brina. She wouldn't let him in until after nine or so, when Petey was asleep, because she thought that it would be hard for Petey to see him. But every night, Tyler arrived at nine and stayed until midnight or so, when Brina kicked him out. Mostly they made love, although once or twice Brina wouldn't. Then Tyler talked. He talked about how much he loved her, how weak he was. About how his weakness didn't affect his love for her, about how hard he'd tried to be faithful. He talked about how much he wanted her back. Brina seemed to listen; but she still wept or cursed him when they did make love. And she always turned away afterward and hunched over, facing the back of the couch and holding herself as if for comfort.

Sometime in the second week of this strange courtship, Meredith called him at work. She sounded tense. There were some problems at the apartment. Could he stop by after work? She'd be home by five-thirty or so.

Tyler couldn't go to Brina's until after nine anyway, so he told Meredith he'd stop by quickly around six.

He drove over in the truck again. He was driving it home regularly now, so he'd be able to get over to Brina's and back easily. Lying on the dashboard was a miniature boot from one of Petey's superhero dolls. Tyler had found it in the glove compartment. He was planning to take it to Brina's later. He'd even thought of a joke he might try on her when he got there, about being a prince looking for the woman who'd fit this shoe. He wasn't sure he would, though, because Brina was several inches taller than he was and so far he'd only imagined two or three tough, sarcastic things she might say in response, having to do with her size.

Meredith had Vivaldi on the radio when he came in. She was wearing jeans and a work shirt, but her makeup was fresh, Tyler could tell. He followed her to the kitchen. She opened the refrigerator and brought out some wine. He watched her lift two glasses down from the shelf. He could see the bumps of her nipples against the light blue shirt. She was thinner than Brina. He took the wine.

She raised her glass. "Cheers," she said, and smiled.

He sipped and set the glass down on the butcher-block counter. He'd installed it three years before. He couldn't help admiring it for a moment. He turned to her. "What's the problem?" he asked.

"No problem," she said. She stepped closer to him. There was a little nick of lipstick on the corner of one of her front teeth. Tyler felt sorry for her.

"I thought there was something wrong," he said.

"Only that I hadn't heard from you," she said, and looked at him. Tyler felt a shrinking inside. "I had a nice time that night."

"Me too," Tyler said, not meeting her eyes. He drank some wine.

"Well?" she said. She cocked her head and smiled flirtatiously at him.

Tyler took a step or two backward. "Look," he said. "I don't know if you knew it or not the other night. I probably should have said something. But I'm married."

She stood very still, but she nodded her head. "I knew."

Then Tyler explained what had happened, how Brina had moved out. She stared at him while he told her, and he watched the determined cheerfulness bleed from her face, the bitter lines creep to the corners of her mouth. She was running her finger again and again around the top of her wineglass. Tyler was telling her how much he loved Brina. Suddenly she smiled at him, a forced, brilliant smile. He fell silent. After a moment she said, "So love her, for Christ's sake." Her upper lip trembled slightly, and a single tear snaked through her makeup. "God knows I wasn't asking you to love *me.*"

Tyler's heart squeezed tight with pity. He closed his eyes and reached for her.

When Brina called from her office, she sounded so crisp and efficient that Tyler for a moment thought it was Meredith again. But then she said, "I'm just calling, Tyler, to tell you where we'll be now. Maryanne's back, so we're going to the Lloyds' for a couple of weeks, while they're gone. Do you have their address?"

"I'm not sure," he said. "I might somewhere, but why don't I write it down, to be safe?"

Brina dictated it to him in her secretarial voice. Tyler's hands trembled as he wrote the numbers and letters. He read it back to her because he was so excited he wasn't sure he'd heard it right. She had called him! She wanted him to know how to get to her. "Thanks, Brina," he said. "Thank you."

The Lloyds had a king-size bed, as Tyler and Brina did at home. The first night Tyler visited Brina there, he slowly and carefully took off all her clothes, then removed his own, and they made love until four in the morning. Before Brina made him leave, he got her to promise to think about moving back home again.

The second night, Tyler brought a bottle of wine and some grass over, but Brina met him at the door wearing an old sweatshirt and jeans. She'd pulled her hair back into a limp ponytail. She told him he couldn't come in. Petey had some stomach bug and was up every half hour or so, vomiting. Tyler wanted to stay, wanted to help with Petey, but Brina was both distracted and absolute.

Driving home, Tyler began to get angry at her rigidity, at the way she insisted that his life should be affected by her principles. He turned out of his way and drove past Meredith's apartment. Her living room lights glowed yellow on the second floor.

She answered the door with the chain on. She was wearing a striped robe and big green puffy slippers. Tyler held up the bottle of wine. "Party time," he said.

She smiled and shut the door. He heard the chain slide off and then she reopened it. She had kicked off the slippers. "I was wondering when you'd get around to coming over again," she said.

Tyler hadn't meant to talk about Brina with her again, but after they made love he felt a resurgence of the anger that had brought him to her apartment in the first place. He told her what Brina had done, making it sound as though it had happened several days before. This time, instead of getting tearful or angry, Meredith took a professional tone. Brina, she offered, was projecting her own anger and fragility onto Petey and using him as a way of punishing Tyler. There were several possible reasons for this, psychodynamically speaking, and Meredith offered one or two.

Tyler knew better than to listen to much of anything she had to say, but he liked speaking about Brina with someone else, liked hearing her name out loud. He felt excited and closer to Brina while he and Meredith were talking about her, and he asked questions to keep the conversation going. He supported her theories with intimate details Brina had told him about her first husband, her childhood. Meredith went to the kitchen to get a cigarette. He watched her walk away from him, small and boyish without any clothes on. "I'm sorry," he said, when she was sitting next to him on the bed again. "I shouldn't talk so much about this. About Brina."

"It's all right. People need to talk about the things that are bothering them."

"But it can't be very much fun for you."

"I don't mind. It's all right."

"It's all right for a while. It shouldn't be for very long, though."

Meredith looked at him as though he were making some sort of promise. "I'll let you know when it starts to bother me."

The next night the phone was ringing when he got back from Brina's. He knew it was Meredith and almost didn't answer it, but the thought of her sitting alone at the other end, listening to the phone ring in his empty apartment, swept him as suddenly and forcefully as a pang of self-pity, and he picked up the receiver.

She was cheerful. She invited him over for a nightcap. Tyler tried to say no, but when she persisted, even began to offer to come to his house, he decided it might be the best thing to go over there briefly.

Tyler saw Meredith five or six times in the next two weeks, sometimes at her apartment, sometimes at his, though they never made love in the bed he shared with Brina. There was something about her sexual greediness that excited him, that gave him an appetite for the tenderness and restraint he had to employ with Brina. And she was the only person he could really talk to about what had happened. He felt all right about it all because, as he told himself, he was always honest with Meredith, he never pretended to her that he didn't want Brina back or wasn't seeing her. In the end, he thought of himself as being faithful to both Meredith and Brina during this period, and he was only tempted once, by a girl he met in a bar on the way home from Brina's one night. She told him she was a law student, and claimed she could also tell his fortune. She took his hand and leaned over it a long time. He could feel her breath warm on his palm. But then she said either the light was bad or he was in sad shape, because she couldn't even find his life line, not to mention his love line and all that other stuff.

Brina and Tyler were lying in the Lloyds' big bed. The Lloyds were supposed to get back from their vacation in five days. Tyler and Brina had avoided talking about this, about where Brina and Petey might go next.

Abruptly, Brina asked if he'd come to dinner the next night.

"What time?" Tyler asked.

"About six or so." There was silence.

Tyler felt his heart thudding as it sometimes did when he'd drunk five or six cups of coffee in one morning. "With Petey," he said.

"He misses you," Brina said. "It just seems dumb, after a while, to keep punishing him because I'm mad at you." Tyler didn't let himself look at Brina, didn't let himself hope. They were lying on their backs, not touching, and he stared intently at the useless nipple-like fixture on the ceiling above him.

"And I'm not so mad at you anymore, Tyler." She sighed. "I guess I see that you can't help yourself—that you're just going to slip every now and then. And that it doesn't mean much of anything to you and me. Or Petey. To who we are as a family, I mean." She had turned on the bed, and Tyler could tell she was looking at him. "But if I think about it too long or hard, I can literally make myself throw up. And I never want to see it or know about it again. Ever." Her voice was like a threat. Tyler nodded his head, and she relaxed again. The light from the candle on the bedside table flickered on the ceiling with the little rush of air from her movement. Tyler lay absolutely still, full of longing for her but afraid to touch her.

"I don't know," she said. Her voice was softer, almost as though she were talking just for herself. "I feel that it's a terrible compromise. Terrible. One I never thought I could make. Or would even be asked to make. I thought of our bodies as being part of each other. It made me feel . . . injured, or damaged. And Petey too. I felt like you broke something that held us all together." Her voice wavered and she was silent for a while. "But then I saw, I guess I saw, that other things really held us together. Or could. Because I do still love you, Tyler." She had turned toward him again. He felt her breath on his shoulder. "What's loving and generous in you. The stuff Petey misses. I miss it too. And it sort of seems fair to me that in the same way you have to struggle with your nature to stay with me, to stay true to me, that I should struggle with mine, with my . . . inflexibility, I guess, to be with you."

Tyler reached out and touched Brina's hand. She responded quickly, passionately, and for the first time since she'd moved out she led them through their lovemaking.

Afterward they talked about when she should move back. Tyler persuaded her that there was no reason to wait until the Lloyds returned. He'd come Saturday with the truck and they could throw everything in and bring her and Petey home. They talked a long time. Tyler fell into a light, then a deep, sleep. Brina didn't wake him until five-thirty. For a moment, opening his eyes in the strange bed, with dawn just outside the windows, Tyler thought he'd stayed too long with some other woman and almost panicked. Then he focused on Brina's half-tender face and his heart slowed down.

Tyler left work early on Friday. He stopped at the five-and-ten and bought a Tonka truck and two new superhero dolls for Petey. Outside Brina's, though, there suddenly seemed something cheap about apologizing to Petey with toys, and he left them in the truck.

He rang the bell. He could hear Petey shout, "It's him!" behind the door. It swung open, and Petey stood there grinning. He was larger than Tyler remembered. He threw himself up and into Tyler's arms. His wiry arms and legs wrapped tightly around Tyler's shoulders and hips. Petey had never embraced Tyler before—no child had—and Tyler was startled and momentarily almost revolted by the animal-like energy in his grip, the sense of his making some claim on Tyler's affection. He realized abruptly how little he'd thought about Petey in the last month or so.

He held Petey awkwardly and patted his narrow, hard back. After a minute, the boy uncoiled himself and dropped from Tyler's body, still smiling up at him, but shyly now, as though he sensed the hesitation in Tyler.

Tyler knew some gesture was required of him. He felt helpless. "My man!" he said, and held out his hands. Petey laughed, and they went through the elaborate hand-slapping routine Tyler had taught him. Then Petey started to tell him about a new game Brina had bought for him. He disappeared down the hall to get it.

Tyler looked up and saw Brina standing in the kitchen doorway. He went to her and held her. There were tears in her eyes and she bowed her head, to rest it on Tyler's shoulder for a minute. "I'm so glad you're here," she whispered.

Petey reappeared, carrying a big flat cardboard box. He asked Brina if he and Tyler could play his game before supper. Brina turned back quickly to the sink so Petey could see only the blank side of her face. "Of course," she said smoothly. Tyler had never realized she might consciously decide which side of her face to show to the world, and he felt a momentary shock, as if of recognition.

The next day, Brina and Petey moved back in with Tyler. As Tyler carried the suitcases, the boxes of Petey's toys up to the apartment, he felt the same sense of hope, the sense that everything could be different, that he'd felt the first time he'd done it. He even tried to carry Brina into the bedroom, but they gave up, laughing, as they had the first time.

That night, while Brina was reading Petey a story, Tyler called Meredith. He'd been nervous all day about the possibility of her telephoning him and Brina's answering, but they'd been out a lot doing errands, getting beer and groceries; and they'd had dinner at a Chinese restaurant, Petey's favorite, to celebrate. Tyler planned to try to see Meredith sometime Monday, for lunch if he could, and tell her as gently as possible what had happened.

She sounded glad to hear from him, although there was an edge to her voice. But when he asked her about getting together Monday, she was silent a moment. Then she said, "Monday? That seems suddenly pretty far away. I mean, I haven't seen you for days."

"Well, things have been happening. We need to talk."

"Let's talk right now. I can talk right now. Why don't you come over?"

"No, I think Monday's best," Tyler said.

"Why?"

"Well, see, I think what's going to happen is that probably . . . well, it's almost definite that Brina's going to move back in." Tyler wasn't aware of lying to Meredith. He was conscious only of a need to spare her feelings.

"Oh, now wait a minute, Tyler. *Wait* a minute," she said. He recognized her tone with relief. She wasn't hurt. She was going to give him advice. "When did all this happen?" she asked.

"Well, it's sort of happening. I mean, we've been talking about it for a couple of days; that's why I haven't called. And I'm going over there tonight."

"So that's it? That's why you can't see me?"

"Right."

"Have you talked to anyone else about this, Tyler? I mean, to get a sense of perspective about what Brina's doing here?"

"No. Just Brina."

"Jesus!"

"What?"

She paused a moment, as though to think of the best way to break bad news. Then she said, "You are so . . . malleable, Tyler. Or gullible or something. I've never met anyone like you." He didn't answer. "Look," she said after a moment. "Where are you now?"

"Why?" Tyler asked, suddenly nervous.

"Just, where are you? Are you home?"

"Yes, but I'm leaving. In just a second. I'm due over there."

"She can wait a few more minutes," Meredith said. "You just sit tight. I'm coming over."

"No!" he said sharply. Then, "No. I need to take off now."

"I'll be there in five minutes, Tyler. You just wait." She hung up.

Tyler sat a few minutes by the telephone, trying to think what to do. He heard Brina reading the story, her voice full of expression, and Petey's bright laughter. He went to the door of Petey's room. Brina was stretched out on Petey's bed, the book propped up on her stomach. Petey leaned against her breast, rhythmically twirling a strand of his hair. Brina finished a sentence and looked up.

"I'm just going to go out for a minute," he said. He knew his voice sounded evasive.

She stared at him. "Out where?" Petey sat up and looked back and forth from one of them to the other, worried by their voices.

Tyler felt a little band of irritation squeeze his stomach. "I'm going to go sit on the front stoop. Okay with you?"

She looked at him a moment more, frowning. Then she lifted her shoulders. "Okay," she said.

Tyler went downstairs and stood on the front steps. It was a warm night and it was still light outside. From the park on the corner he could hear the sounds of a ball game. An old couple three doors down had brought folding chairs outside and were sitting on the sidewalk, talking and surveying the empty street. Tyler put his hands in his pockets and looked first one way down the street and then the other. He sat down. Minutes passed. He felt almost sick. He debated walking to the corner to head Meredith off, but worried that for some reason she might come from the other direction and ring the bell before he could get back. He suddenly recalled her frosted hair, the dark nail polish she wore, things he knew that Brina would think cheap. A window opened and closed above him. Somewhere, someone called a wandering child to a slow rhythm: "Daaavid. Daaavid."

Meredith drove up. She got quickly out of the car, walked around behind it and came to stand in front of him. She smiled. "Hi," she said.

Tyler stood up. "Look, I've gotta get going," he said. "This really isn't a good time for me."

She looked at the old couple, who were watching them. "Let's just go inside for a few minutes, Tyler," she said. "I think I really need to talk to you about this."

Her voice was firm and authoritative, and Tyler felt again the irritation he'd felt before with Brina, more sharply this time. Who were these women, who thought they could run his life?

"Can't swing it," he said. He was startled by the absoluteness in his own voice.

She looked at him. "This isn't like you, Tyler." He shrugged. She shook her head. "I just have to tell you, Tyler, that I think she's done a real number here."

"We're married, Meredith. She doesn't have to do any number for us to live together."

She looked at him, her eyes widening. They were a lighter color than he'd thought. "I really can't believe this," she said. "I just cannot believe it."

Tyler felt as though he were being accused of breaking some promise. "I never told you I was leaving Brina," he said.

"You never said so, no," she said. "But what were all those conversations we had? I mean, someone just doesn't *talk* that way."

He looked at her blankly.

"Tyler," she said. There was pleading in her voice and her lower eyelids suddenly shimmered with tears. Tyler hated this. She saw him weakening and reached up to put her hand on his arm.

Tyler had just begun to pull away gently, when he heard the crash behind him. He turned around. Brina stood in the lobby between the building's two glass doors. She stared through the outer glass door at Meredith and Tyler on the stoop. She held an empty tray crookedly, and around her feet on the tiled floor were green shards of broken bottle glass, an overturned bowl, a bubbly pool of what must have been beer. Tyler stared in at her. Slowly, he raised his hands and put them on the glass door. She looked back out at him for a long moment, her whole face expressionless. Then her lips parted, moved a little as though she were whispering something; and the muscles began to pull and shift in the live side of her face. Tyler stepped closer to the door. But as he stared through the glass wall at her, she turned away from him. Now all he could see in Brina's face was her vacant serenity as she looked down at the mess that lay around her feet.

# Appropriate Affect

Grandma Frannie was a tall, slim woman, stooped now, who had been pretty before all her children were born. She still had a beautiful smile, with all her own teeth. It was sweet and sad, perhaps even reproachful, and she had used it for years to shame the family into orderly compliance. She had met Henry Winter before she finished library school, and brought to her marriage all the passion she had once lavished on the Dewey decimal system. In passion, she was disappointed. Henry was a rigid and unimaginative man, though a dutiful lover. She was pregnant within two months of the wedding, and within five years she had four daughters, Maggie, Laura, Frieda and Martha.

No one escaped the bright beam of Grandma Frannie's love. At eighty-six, she still sent birthday presents to every grandchild and great-grandchild. She remembered who was married to whom, and even who was living with whom, what his name was, and what he did. Although it didn't really matter what anyone did.

Her love leapt all hurdles. Her oldest grandson, Martin, who had a coming out party within a month of moving to San Francisco, had dedicated his first volume of poetry to Frannie. His mother cried when he told her he'd sent Frannie a copy, but Frannie kept it in plain view, on the coffee table in the living room. When Martin's mother saw it there, she didn't comment. She figured Frannie probably didn't even know what it was about. And the Christmas after Fred showed up at a family Thanksgiving party with a black stripper, Frannie sent a card that brought love "to that pretty Tanya" and a gift (small, because she wasn't family) from the church bazaar.

"Christ," said Louisa, Frieda's youngest and a graduate student in psychology, "you can't be a black sheep in this family even if you want." It was true. The steady pressure of Grandma's love reduced them all, eventually, to gray normality. Even Julian, who was in prison in Joliet, Illinois, for forgery, wrote her regularly.

Frannie and Henry lived in Connecticut in a large frame house built on a hill. It had once overlooked an abandoned orchard where wizened little apples grew. Ten years before, a developer had leveled the field and built row on row of identical two-story gray town houses with fake mansard roofs.

Henry and Frannie's house was a faded salmon pink that was gently peeling, and here and there a shutter had fallen off and never been replaced. It was darkened by overgrown cedars in the front yard which reached above the roof for sunlight. The front porch listed slightly, but Bob Hancock, Laura's son-in-law, had jumped up and down on it and it held. It was pronounced safe for Frannie and Henry for the time being.

All the children wanted them to move to the retirement community nearby, but Henry couldn't bear to think of it. He loved the ornate woodwork and soot-streaked wallpaper, the dark furniture inherited from his mother, and the threadbare Oriental rugs.

One Sunday afternoon, an hour or so after their return from the Congregational church, Henry was watching football on television. Frannie came into the living room to tell him that dinner was ready. It was in the middle of the third quarter and that irritated Henry. Because he was slightly deaf and had the television on loud, he didn't hear her coming and that irritated him even more. She stepped suddenly into his line of vision and turned the set off. She shouted, "Dinner, Henry," at him, and smiled her warm, browbeaten smile.

Henry stood up. "There's no need to shout," he said. "What's more, I'm not ready for dinner and I won't be for a good long while. The Sabbath was made for man, madam, not man for the Sabbath." And he walked right over to the TV set and turned it back on.

She said something to him, but he ignored her, so she started her long, slow shuffle back to the kitchen.

Henry turned the set off about forty-five minutes later and started toward the kitchen himself. His walk was brisker and more steady than Frannie's. He stopped abruptly when he rounded the doorway to the dining room. Frannie's legs were sticking straight out from behind the highboy on the floor. He felt a numbed panic as he approached her. She was sitting up, wedged in the corner between the highboy and the wall. Her face was white and agonized. Her mouth had dropped open and her eyes were closed.

"My dear!" Henry said, bending over her stiffly from the waist. He saw her lips move slightly as though she were trying to talk. Her left arm rested uselessly on the floor and her right was somehow bent behind her. Henry reached down and tried to lift her up, but he only managed to slide her forward slightly. Her head lolled back and smacked the wall. Henry cried out. He straightened and started into the kitchen. Halfway to the telephone, with his arms already lifting to take off the receiver and dial, he turned and went back to her. He bent down again.

"I'll be right back, my darling," he said very loudly and clearly, as though she were the deaf one. She made no sign that she'd heard. He went back and placed the call.

* * *

No one answered when the ambulance driver rang the bell, so the men walked in with the stretcher. They looked around the dark, empty front hall and then heard a murmuring voice from the room on their right, the dining room. Henry had pulled a chair over next to Frances, and he was sitting in it, holding her hand across his knees and patting it, talking softly to her.

When the ambulance driver was only a few steps away, Henry saw him and stopped talking. He stood up. "Sir, my name is Henry Winter and this is my wife," he said. He began to explain the circumstances under which he'd found her, but the men were already lifting her onto the stretcher and strapping her in, giving loud instructions to each other.

"You coming in the ambulance, Pop?" the driver asked as he picked up his end of the stretcher.

"What say?" asked Henry, turning his head so his good ear was nearer the driver.

"Are you coming with us?" the driver yelled.

"Ah! Much obliged, but I'll follow in my car," said Henry, and he went to get his hat and coat.

"Christ!" the driver said a minute later as they hoisted Frannie into the truck. "Can you imagine them letting an old guy like that have a license?"

In the days following Frannie's stroke, different children, grandchildren and great-grandchildren came and went in the house. As though it were an old country hotel getting ready for the season, rooms that had been shut up for years were opened, mouse droppings and dead insects were swept up and mattresses turned over. Frannie's daughters ransacked the bedding box and clucked to each other about the down puffs and heavy linen sheets with hand stitching that you would think Mother might have handed down by now.

For the first three days they took turns going in one at a time to sit by Frannie in intensive care. They got permission to have a member of the family stay by her straight through the night. The third night it was her granddaughter Charlotte's turn.

The overhead lights were off in the hospital room, but a white plastic nipple plugged into the wall socket next to Frannie's bed glowed like a child's night light and Charlotte could see the shape of her grandmother's skinny body under the bedclothes. She didn't like to look at Gram's face, so embryonic and naked without her glasses, her hair uncombed for three days and her mouth slack. Instead she looked at the sac of IV fluid with its plastic umbilicus running into Gram's bruised arm. Or she held Gram's freckled hand, which lay alongside the mound of bones under the sheets; or she slept; or wept. She rubbed her hands up and down her slightly thickening waist and cried as she thought of life and death; of Gram about to die, and of the baby, her third, taking life inside her own body.

She had tried to talk about this to her younger sister, Louisa, the afternoon before at Frannie and Henry's house, but Louisa had been irritable. Louisa was always irritable when Charlotte cried. "Oh, spare us, why don't you," she'd said, chopping onions for stew. Her knife whacked the board rapidly, like a burst of gunfire. "Next you'll be going on about reincarnation."

Charlotte blew her nose loudly into a Kleenex, and wiped her lower lids carefully so the mascara wouldn't smear. Grandma Frannie stirred slightly and swung her head toward Charlotte. Her mouth closed with a smacking sound and opened again. Charlotte leaned toward the bed, grabbing the steel railings that boxed her grandmother in.

"Gram?" she whispered. She cleared her throat. "Gram?" Her grandmother's eyes snapped open and stared wildly for a second. Then the lids seemed to grow heavy and they drooped again.

Charlotte stood up and put one hand on her grandmother's shoulder. The other hand rested on her own belly. At her touch, her grandmother's eyes opened again and she frowned and seemed to try to fix Charlotte in focus with the anxious intensity of a newborn.

"Gram? Do you hear me?" Charlotte said. "Do you hear me?"

After a few seconds' pause, Grandma Frannie nodded, a slow swaying of her frizzy head.

"Do you know me?" asked Charlotte. Gram shut her lips and tightened them and frowned hard at Charlotte.

"It's Charlotte, Grandma," she said, and started to weep again. Her right hand was furiously rubbing her belly. She was already thinking of how she would tell the others of this moment. She leaned over and put her face close to her grandmother's.

"It's Charlotte, Grandma. Do you know me?"

Again her grandmother moved her head slightly, up and down. Her lips quivered with some private effort.

"Oh, Grandma, I wanted you to know. I'm going to have a baby." Tears ran down Charlotte's face and plopped onto the neatly folded sheet covering her grandmother's chest. "I'm going to have another baby, Gram."

There was no change in the intense frown on Grandma Frannie's face, but her mouth opened. Charlotte leaned closer still and Grandma Frannie's breath was horrible in her face. Frannie's lips worked and her breathing was shallow and fast.

"The. Nasty. Man," she whispered.

Charlotte reported to the doctors and the family that Grandma Frannie had waked in the night and had spoken. When they asked, as they did eagerly and repeatedly, what she had said, Charlotte would only say that she hadn't been herself. Her cousin Elinore thought Charlotte was being "a bit of a snot" not to tell, trying to rivet all that attention on herself. Charlotte felt everyone's irritation with her all the next day. Frannie was fluttering delicately in and out of consciousness and muttered only incoherent phrases as the nurses changed her bedding or inserted another IV. But Charlotte still tearfully refused to tell what it was Grandma had said to her, although she insisted that Grandma had spoken clearly. "God, you'd think it was her mantra," Louisa said.

After Charlotte heard Grandma Frannie speak, the family came by twos and threes for several days. Slowly Frannie began to recognize them, calling out their names as they walked in. Sometimes she couldn't seem to say the name and then she'd spell it aloud, carefully and often correctly. It was a small hospital, and the doctors and nurses came to know the family as they sat in little clusters in the lounge or cafeteria, waiting for a turn to see Frannie.

In the evening at the house, there were always nine or ten around the dinner table. Henry felt an almost unbearable joy sometimes when he was called in to the extended table covered with a white linen cloth. The china and glassware glittered. The tureens and platters that had come down from his parents were heaped with food like creamed onions and scalloped potatoes, food Henry hadn't eaten at home in years, except at Thanksgiving or Christmas.

They talked animatedly at the table of what Gram had said or done that day. Everyone had a favorite story he liked to tell. Frannie had asked Elinore to get the bedpan, but called it a perambulator. She had clearly asked Maggie if she was going to die and cried when Maggie told her she would not, that she was getting better. She rambled on and on to Emily, her youngest grandchild, who was down from Smith for the weekend. She talked about apple trees and she had said, "I think of all those trees gone, don't you know, the apples, all cut down. Well, that's the way. All those trees." Emily had sat in the darkened room and stroked her hand. "Why would they do a thing like that?" Grandma Frannie had asked, and Emily had said, honestly, that she didn't know. Then Grandma Frannie had said, "Those assholes!" but Emily was sure she had meant to say "apples," so she didn't repeat that part.

Henry told over and over how he had found her and called for the ambulance. He didn't tell the whole truth. He said, "My dearest was in the kitchen making dinner. I sat in the corner of the living room, you see, watching football—it was, I believe, the Los Angeles Rams that day, but I could be wrong—and when the game was over, I walked back towards the kitchen to inquire about dinner, and as I came around the corner, what do you think

I saw?" He would wait here however long it took some listener to ask, "What?"

"*There* was my darling sitting on the floor with her legs protruding out from behind the highboy that Auntie gave us for a wedding present." He would go on, detailing every step of the process of getting Frannie to the hospital, and making himself sound very heroic.

The group staying at the house shrank and stabilized somewhat after it became clear that Frannie was going to survive. Maggie stayed on with Henry to take care of him, and Charlotte, who lived nearby, often came for part of the day while her children were in school. Sometimes she returned later with them and her husband, to have dinner with Maggie and Henry.

Frequently, one of the other children or grandchildren would arrive for a day or two. Michael stopped in one night with his entire band, Moonshot, and a few of their girlfriends on the way to a gig in the Berkshires. Maggie told everyone later, "Who knows who was with whom. I just told them where the bedrooms were and shut my eyes."

Grandma Frannie made extraordinary progress. She was having therapy with a walker and physically she had recovered almost completely, except for a dragging in her left leg. Most of her powers of speech had returned. But she still had trouble with an occasional word and when she was tired she would lose track of where she was and to whom she was speaking and drift off to other places and times. Like a baby, she napped three or four times a day.

One afternoon, Henry went in alone to visit her. She was asleep. Her mouth puffed out with each exhalation and she snored faintly. Henry stood in the open doorway and tried to engage some of the passing hospital staff in conversation. His loud voice woke Frannie up.

"Henry!" she called to him.

He turned. "Oh, my dear, now you're awake, and looking so well today, so very well." He leaned over and kissed her cheek.

"Graphics," she said.

"Eh?"

She bit her lip and looked angry. "Now I didn't mean that," she said. "Fetch me my . . . you know." She pointed to her nose. The marks of her glasses were like permanent bluish stains on either side of the bridge. "They're somewhere or other in that coffin there," and she gestured at the stand by her bed.

Henry opened the drawer and got her glasses out. He started to help her put them on, but she waved his hands away and hooked them over her ears herself.

"My love," Henry began, seating himself by her bed.

But she cut him off. "Where *were* you?" she asked.

"Why, my dear, I just arrived, but you were asleep so I stood by the door. . . ."

"Not likely!" she snapped, and behind her glasses her eyes glinted malevolently at him.

"Very well, my love," he said in an injured tone, resolved to be patient. The doctors had told him it was a miracle she had survived at all, and besides, Henry couldn't forget the shame of his behavior to her in the moments before her stroke. Worse yet, he found himself hoping she would never recover fully enough to recall it herself, to blame him or tell the children.

"I heard you down there in that other room," Frannie said, slowly and carefully.

"Now, Frannie, you must stay calm."

She shut her eyes and seemed for a moment to relax or to be asleep. Then her eyes opened and she smiled. "Yes, I'm not well. Not a bit well."

"But you're getting better."

Her lips labored, as though choosing the exact position they needed to be in to form the next word. "The children were here."

"That's right, dear."

"Maggie. And Frieda. And Martha. And that other."

"Laura? She couldn't come. She wasn't here."

"Not Laura," she said irritably. "Not one of mine. That other."

"Louisa? Charlotte?"

"Yes! That one." She smiled in satisfaction. A moment later she said, "Did I tell you the children were here?"

"Yes, you just did, my love. You just said that." And he laughed loudly at her.

Her eyes narrowed behind the bifocals. Her mouth tensed into an angry line. A nurse walked in briskly.

"Ah, here comes that . . ." She stopped.

"It's Nurse Gorman, Mrs. Winter. Just checking your blood pressure again."

"Again? You have nothing superior to do?" Something funny in her sentence made Frannie shake her head angrily.

"I just wanted to get another reading 'cause it's been a few hours, honey." She pumped up the band around Frannie's skinny arm, squeezing the loose flesh close to the bone. "Your wife is my favorite patient, Mr. Winter. She's a doll."

"Eh?" said Henry.

"Your wife is doing well," yelled the nurse. She was tall and wore glasses and very red lipstick.

"Oh, I know, yes, thanks," said Henry.

After the nurse left, Frannie closed her eyes for a while and seemed to sleep again. Henry looked at a copy of *Newsweek* he'd picked up in the lobby.

"Oh, you're still here." She labored over the words.

"Yes, my love," he said, and patted her hand.

"Why don't you just go down there. If you want to. Go right on down. To your little nurse."

Henry frowned.

"I heard you down there. Yes. The children, probably. Thought it was just me again. Making that noise. But I knew just what it was with that Mrs. Sheffield." She said this very slowly and precisely. "Fuck-ing Mrs. Sheffield."

Henry started and withdrew his hand.

"Always that. Mrs. Sheffield. When I wanted some other nurse, but oh, no, you had to have her. Again. Sneaking off down the hall. Did you think I couldn't hear? You? I knew just what it was. I heard you."

"You're upset, Frances. You—you should sleep."

"Yes. Sleep. Don't you wish. I saw you looking at her. As soon as I sleep you'll go off. Down the hall again. Why couldn't we have some other nurse? I didn't want Mrs. Sheffield again." Her voice had become plaintive.

Henry stood up.

Frances began to cry. Her face crumpled into bitter lines. "I don't want her. There's too many children here, and you. Always sneaking around with her, making those noises down the hall. Yes, go. Go on. I know where you're . . . you're going."

Henry drove home slowly. He didn't notice the line of cars forming behind him and he didn't hear the honking. The sun was low and pink in the Connecticut sky. He was remembering Mrs. Sheffield, whose eyes had bulged out slightly so that the whites showed all the way around the iris and made Henry think of nipples sitting round and staring in the middle of her breasts. She was quiet and solemn as she performed her duties after Maggie's birth and she wouldn't sit with him at meals. He had known what he wanted from her when he wrote to hire her again for the second child. After that she had come and stayed with them at each birth, and Frannie, he thought, had never known. Mrs. Sheffield was small and plump, with dark hair, and he had been right, her nipples did sit exactly in the middle of her small breasts, unlike his wife's, which drooped down and leaked milk at his mouth's pull for years on end.

When he got home, Henry called the doctor and explained that he thought his presence was distressing to his wife, and with his permission Henry wouldn't come in for a bit. The doctor was surprised that Henry thought he needed permission to stay away.

And now each person who visited Frannie came to a point in telling how she was doing where he or she would fall silent and then say in a perplexed tone that Grandma Frannie was still not really herself. In little groups of two and three they discussed her and they agreed that they wouldn't have believed Grandma Frannie even knew the meaning of half the words she was using. She told Charlotte's husband that Henry didn't know the first thing about fucking. She said "fucking." "In and out," she said. "That was his big idea. I hope you take a little more time and care. And if you don't know what's up," she said, "there's no shame in asking."

She told Maggie that she had thought she would die when they were all little. She said she'd spent fifteen years "up to my elbows in runny yellow shit. Not one of you children turned out a well-formed stool until you were doing it on your own."

Maggie had blushed and spoken to her as though she were a child. "Be nice, Mother," she'd said, nervously smiling.

"Oh, nice, nice!" said Grandma Frannie. "I know very well how to be nice."

Like Henry, the children and grandchildren began to think of reasons why they couldn't visit. Maggie still went once a day, but most of the time the others stayed away. Late one night Maggie called her husband long-distance in Pennsylvania. She stood in her flannel nightgown in the hall and sobbed softly into the phone so Henry wouldn't hear her. "I can't imagine where she ever heard that kind of language. I almost wished she'd died rather than end up like this."

A few weeks after this, when Frannie began to get better, the doctors called it the return of "appropriate affect." Maggie sent out a family letter saying: "Mother's coming around. She's practically back to normal except for forgetting a few words and we're planning on a homecoming party soon."

And later: "Mother seems just about okay now. Sends her love to everyone and asks about you all. She can't remember who visited and who didn't, but she's talking normally now, thank goodness. For those who can come, we'll bring her home February 16 in the early afternoon and the doctor says a very short party would be all right."

*　　*　　*

Snow had fallen the night of the fifteenth, but the sixteenth was bright and cold. Frannie's daughters and granddaughters took charge of lunch. One of the sons-in-law put the extra leaf in the table again and took three of the smaller children out to shovel the walk. They ran in and out all morning, bringing cold air and snow into the front hall. "Here, here," Henry said crossly. "In or out. I'm not paying to heat all outdoors."

Someone brought a towel and left it by the front door to mop up the puddles of melting snow. Charlotte's husband lugged two high chairs up from the basement, washed off the dust and cobwebs, and set them at corners of the table.

The chime of the metal shovel ringing on concrete outside, the banging of the front door, the good smells from the kitchen, the table gleaming with silver, made it seem like a dozen Christmases they'd shared in the past. But there was a subdued anxiousness among the adults and several tense abbreviated conversations. Maggie said over and over to people, "Really, she's quite all right now." Henry was surly and spent the morning watching TV or scolding his great-grandchildren.

At one o'clock, Bob Hancock's car swung up the driveway. His oldest boy, Nick, jumped out from the far side and extracted a walker from the back seat. He brought it around to the door Bob was opening at the foot of the walk. Frannie rose slowly out of the car and Nick put the walker down in front of his great-grandmother. The children who were outside danced around her and their muffled shouts brought the family in the house to the windows. "She's home! She's home!" they cried. Henry rose and went to the window.

Slowly, with Nick at one elbow and Bob at the other, Frannie made her way across the shoveled, sanded walk. Her entourage of great-grandchildren in bright nylon snowsuits leapt around her. She was watching her feet, so Henry couldn't see her face. Charlotte had gone to the hospital two days before to give her a permanent, and her hair was immobilized in rigid waves on her head, though the wind made her coat flap.

She turned at the bottom of the porch stairs and Bob came to face her. Holding each other's hands like partners in some old court dance, they stepped sideways up the stairs. Then the children burst open the front door, yelling and stomping the snow off their feet and taking advantage of the excitement to dance around in the front hall without having to remove their boots. Frannie shuffled in and looked around at her family gathered in an irregular circle in the hallway. Charlotte fished a Kleenex out of her maternity smock and several others wiped at their eyes.

"Where's Henry?" Frannie asked. Henry felt a slight constriction in his chest, but he pushed past his children and grandchildren and stood before her. "Here I am, my darling," he said. She looked at him a moment. Then she smiled her sad smile and raised her face to be kissed. Gratefully, he put his lips to hers.

The children yelled and danced, the adults broke into applause. Henry said softly, "It's wonderful to see you yourself again, Frances."

Grandma Frannie looked at him and then at her clapping family. She raised her hands slightly as though to ward off the noise, and for a moment her face registered confusion. But the applause continued.

Then she seemed to realize what they wanted from her. Unassisted and shaky, she stepped forward and smiled again. Slowly she bowed her head, as though to receive the homage due a long and difficult performance.

# Slides

There were seven slides, and Georgia was naked in all of them. She had been slender and attractive, although in a monochromatic way. Her hair was dirty blond, her skin had a beige tone, and her eyes were light brown. But her small breasts were round and tilted up at the nipples, and her hips, which were later described by a woman selling an exercise program at the YWCA pool as her "problem area," were then nicely curved, merely full.

Georgia's ex-husband, David, had taken all the slides early in their marriage. He hadn't even asked permission before he took the first one. He had been sitting on the secondhand couch in their first apartment. He was wearing shorts, and fiddling with a camera they'd been given as a wedding present. Georgia had walked naked into the room, carrying *Amy Vanderbilt's Book of Etiquette,* also a wedding present, to read David the section on thank-you notes. She was wearing new glasses. They were horn-rimmed and businesslike, and she thought they made her look older for her first job, a teaching assistantship in political science. They'd come back from their honeymoon three days earlier, and the shape of Georgia's bikini seemed imprinted on her brown body in silvery flesh. The white band circling her hips made her dark bush shocking. Just as she looked up to begin to read to him, David took her picture, fully frontal.

"You bastard!" she said. "I hope that thing isn't loaded."

"Would I have wasted a flash if it weren't loaded?" David was grinning.

"Give me the film." Although Georgia felt flattered, she was angry too, and her voice was hard. David kept smiling. He held the camera away from her. "I mean it, David. Give me the film."

"I can't, George. It's on a roll with a lot of other good stuff."

"Well, you're not developing it anyway, so you might as well give it to me." She was stretching across him, trying not to touch his body with hers and still grab the camera.

He reached up and held her breast, which was bobbling inches from his face, with his free hand. "George, this is silly." He licked her.

She pulled away, glaring at him. Her nipple, where his warm tongue had made it wet, tingled with cold. She covered it with her hand.

David was surprised at the anger in her face. He asked her more seriously, "Why don't you want it developed?"

She sat down at a distance from him on the couch. "Because I don't want some bunch of jerks at the developing place leering at my body, I guess."

"But that's not the way it works, George. They don't develop them by hand anymore. They don't even look at them most of the time. It's a purely mechanical process." David wasn't at all sure of this, but he knew Georgia would take his word for it. "Let's just send it in with the rest and see how it comes out."

Georgia was convinced, as she frequently was then, by the sweet reasonableness in David's tone. When the slides came back, David borrowed a projector from a friend who worked in the biology lab with him, and she sat down with him in the darkened room to watch the images slip by them. Pictures of the Caribbean island on which they'd honeymooned cast green and blue shadows over their faces. Georgia had made popcorn, but David wouldn't touch it until the show was over because he didn't want to get grease on the slides.

He had taken most of the pictures. The new camera had excited him. He had brought along on their honeymoon all the literature that had come with it, and kept it spread out over the bureau and bed in the little stone cottage they'd stayed in. Georgia was irritated at his sloppiness, which she had never noticed before. But every time they went out, the black maid would come in and neatly stack the literature again on the bedside table; the sheets would be changed, the bed would be taut.

Georgia had taken only a few pictures of David. In one, he was asleep on the beach. Georgia had been sitting by his feet when she snapped it, so they loomed large in the foreground. His small head lolled to one side in the distance, mouth open.

"Very attractive, George," David commented, and pushed the button.

"This popcorn is terrific," Georgia said by way of apology. "Don't you want me to shove a few greasy little kernels into your mouth for you?" David declined.

Finally, in the midst of the honeymoon shots, David pushed the button and Georgia came on, naked, duck-footed, holding the Amy Vanderbilt as though it were the text for a lesson she was giving. The flash gleamed doubly from the lenses of her glasses. Georgia stopped chewing for a moment. David cleared his throat, but said nothing. He pushed the focus button several times, as though in hopes of improving the picture. The mechanism whined. The projector's fan whirred steadily in the silence between them.

"Well," said Georgia finally, reaching for another handful. "It sure makes that picture I took of you look like great PR."

"I'll admit it isn't particularly *erotic,*" David began.

"Erotic! Anyone who could even maintain an erection in the presence of that picture deserves some sort of award. God! Switch it. And I'm not saving any of this popcorn for you, either." In spite of herself, Georgia was profoundly disappointed in the slide, in her lack of grace or beauty in it. She felt a sudden flash of hateful anger for David, as though he were responsible for the way she looked to herself.

When they were through with the slides, David packed up the projector, putting each part with satisfaction into its Styrofoam casing. Then he made some more popcorn and came to sit by Georgia. They sat together in the half light, both remembering their honeymoon. The things they remembered were quite different, but the memories made each of them similarly happy. They kissed, sliding their buttered lips together, and after a while made love on the couch.

They lay silent together. Georgia was almost asleep. David whispered, "George, let me take another picture of you."

"Oh, David, *why?*" Georgia moaned in sleepy irritation.

"Because that picture *is* awful, Georgia, and I'd like a good one, a beautiful one." He leaned up on one elbow and stroked her arm. His words came slowly and with effort, as they always did when he was most serious. She abandoned her annoyance and tried to listen. "I'd like to take a picture that somehow reflects how I'm feeling right now. That shows how much I love you. Let me."

Georgia was overwhelmingly sleepy. She trusted David's tone of voice, so she agreed. He got up carefully, easing his leg out from under hers. He found the camera, and took the picture as she slept on the couch. Her eyelids tightened reflexively when the flash went off, but she didn't awake.

Over the next two years, before she got pregnant with Jeff, he took the other five pictures. Each time she consented, and each time she was disturbed and saddened by the slide, though she always pretended to laugh at the graceless young girl half-reclining on the bed or sitting stiffly in the bathtub. She knew she couldn't talk about her real feelings to David. It would mean acknowledging some different, private idea she had of herself, an idea that his satisfaction with the slides told her he didn't share.

The last time David photographed her, she was furious. They had just finished making love, in bed this time, and he got up almost immediately afterward, announcing, "I'm getting the camera."

She sat up silent and sullen, glaring at him while he worked the camera, and then she burst out. She accused him of relating to life exclusively through machines. She accused him of being unable to value her or appreciate her sexually without some sort of record of it. She accused him of caring more for the making of the fucking record than he did for her feelings. She told him she never wanted him to photograph her again.

It was the best picture he had ever taken of her; the only one in which she looked completely unselfconscious.

When David and Georgia got divorced, Georgia got custody of Jeff because her schedule was more flexible and she could be with him more. Of their possessions, she wanted only the things that would make Jeff feel at home and a few odd items she'd been especially attached to. And in every case over which there was potential disagreement, they sat down and discussed, reasonably and fairly, the relative merits of each claim.

David, for instance, initially thought he should have the stereo system, since he had spent weeks sifting through catalogues and magazine articles to select the components, and was always the one to fix or adjust it. But Georgia, sitting with her bare feet tucked under her in her favorite chair in the living room (the only piece of furniture from the living room she wanted), pointed out that she was the one of the two who liked music, who actually listened to the stereo. What David liked about it, she argued in the persuasive voice she'd learned to use in classroom disagreements—a voice very like the patient tone David had used with her in their courtship and early marriage—were its mechanical qualities, which could be replaced by any other complex mechanical object. It seemed to her that it was she who cared for its more essential quality, its ability to reproduce music.

While she made her argument, her hands were in constant motion; and David, lying on their expensive tweed sofa with a coffee mug resting on his chest, watched the sequence of familiar configurations, gestures she had made thousands of times before: the touch up to push her hair back, the fingers curling in onto her breast, the two-handed diamond shape in the air in front of her. They were part of her enjoyment of the process of making her argument. David watched her intently.

When she ended, she was smiling. "Don't you think?" she asked. She held her right hand out, palm up, fingers spread. In the long silence that followed, she could see on David's face a mixture of affection and disgust. She felt caught in a habitual weakness and was, somehow, ashamed of herself.

"Yes," said David finally. "Of course you're right."

A few days later, David, who had been sorting through the slides to divide them up, came in to ask her if she knew where "the nudies," as Georgia had called them, were.

Georgia said that of course she'd taken them.

David said he thought she hated them.

"I do," Georgia said.

"Then what do you want them for?"

"It isn't really wanting them. It's more like putting them away with my things."

"Well, *I* really want them."

She looked up at him sharply. She was kneeling on the floor by her file drawer, organizing its contents for packing. She wore her glasses, and a faded plaid shirt. "What for?" she asked.

"I like them. I took them." His tone was sharp, possessive. As though he heard this himself, he stopped and started again, in a calmer, more reasonable voice. "I'd like to have them to remind me of a time when we were happier."

The change in tone made Georgia think David was trying to con her. "That's a little schmaltzy, isn't it? Don't you mean you'd like something to jerk off to?"

"If I wanted to jerk off, those pictures are the last ones I'd use!"

"You're not kidding." She slammed the file drawer shut. "Because you're not getting them."

"Now just a fucking second," he said. "I thought the deal was that everything we owned was both of ours until we agreed on whose it was."

"This is different." She rose and started to walk past him out of the room. From somewhere distantly in the apartment, Jeff's television program droned. David grabbed her arm, and she swung to face him. "How is this different? I like those pictures; you hate them. They mean something to me; they mean nothing—"

"They're *of me,* you asshole." She was almost shouting. "They're of my body. They belong to me."

"I missed just a few steps in that impeccable logic."

They stood in silence, looking at each other, both breathing rapidly, wondering what could ever have seemed dear or worth loving in the other.

"All right, then," said Georgia. "Let me just say that I can imagine how you might use the slides, and I don't want them used that way."

"How do you imagine I'd use them?"

"I imagine you'd show them. Isn't that what people do with slides? I imagine you'd show them. I imagine that with some reason."

Georgia referred to an evening they'd spent a year or two before with David's college roommate. They had all had too much to drink. Georgia had felt flirtatious and gay with this man who had known her before she became the overworked academic matron she felt she was now. At dinner, the subject of the slides had come up. David and Eliot, high and sexually titillated at the idea in a way that disgusted Georgia, had tried to talk her into a showing. At first they misunderstood her refusal, thinking it was part of the teasing tone she'd used earlier. She slowly withdrew into a cold rage, and had finally gone into the bedroom, telling them they could do what they fucking well pleased. Eliot had left a short while later, and in his Christmas card hadn't mentioned the dinner.

Now David was stung. His face turned white and his voice was low. "I didn't show the slides to Eliot."

"But you would've if I hadn't been there."

"You *weren't* there. You left, if you recall."

"Ah, but by then you were so embarrassed that you couldn't show them. No, I can see exactly how it'd happen if I weren't there. You have a few of the boys over, you're talking about women." She was crying now, but unable to stop. "You have a few words to say about me, this broad you used to be married to, and then—hey!—you remember those slides, and pretty soon you're getting out the old screen and projector, two of your favorite mechanical devices—"

"*Okay,* Georgia."

"But that's not the *point,* David. The main point is what a bummer it would be. The main point is how everyone would just *not* be turned on at all. And as soon as the lights went on, everyone would have to go. It would *ruin* your party, David."

"Okay, George." He wasn't looking at her face, blotchy and distorted with self-pity.

"And I'd *hate* to ruin your party," she persisted helplessly.

He turned, and with a long motion of his arm that involved his whole body, swept her desk clear of the carefully organized stacks of paper.

"*Keep* the fucking pictures!" he yelled as he walked out of the room.

It was eight years later, when Georgia was thirty-seven, that she met Peter Anderson. By then she hardly thought about David anymore unless they were making some special arrangement having to do with Jeff. She never spoke of him. If someone asked about her ex-husband, and hardly anyone did, she was as vague as possible. She felt that in divorcing herself from him, she'd cut away all those things he'd brought into her life that she didn't like; and all the things about herself, developed in response to him, that had troubled her. She was happier with herself now.

She met Peter one evening when she was out with friends, celebrating the acceptance of an article of hers for publication. Peter was a friend of theirs, and they'd waved him over from across the dining room. Georgia was a little drunk, glowing with accomplishment, and very outgoing.

Three days later, he called. It was a cold, clear Sunday. Georgia was by herself, drinking coffee and reading the *Times*. She wore a heavy bathrobe and two pairs of socks, and sat in front of the opened oven door, the paper scattered in heaps on the floor around her. All weekend she had felt immobilized by loneliness and the cold weather, and she almost ran to the phone when it rang. Although she remembered meeting him, she had trouble recalling what Peter Anderson looked like. But he even remembered that she had a child about the age of one of his. (She winced. She had dragged Jeff into this drunken flirtation?) His children were in town for the weekend, and about to go ice skating. He wondered if maybe . . .

No, she said. Jeff was away, with his father. And anyway, he didn't like—no, *she* didn't like using him as a way to meet people. "It's too much like walking dogs," she said.

There was a silence. "I understand," he said. "Thanks anyway."

The next Friday night, on her way to get Jeff from a soccer game, Georgia stopped at the liquor store and picked up a half gallon of cheap white wine. At supper, Jeff was in a cheerful, expansive mood, and she relaxed, listening to him talk about his soccer game, then about some kids who got caught having a distance contest at the urinals. He told her three new jokes he'd learned, and Georgia laughed happily at them. But as soon as he went into the living room to do his homework, she felt alone again. She sat down at the table, still covered with dirty dishes, and poured herself a glass of wine. She drank it fast, making patterns with her fingers in the crumbs left from the garlic bread. The spaghetti sauce had hardened to a deep brown on the plates. She had no special plans for the weekend except to work on the revision of her thesis and to prepare for Monday's class. The two days stretched out long and cold and empty. Maybe she'd take Jeff ice skating Saturday. Then she remembered Peter and her rudeness to him and looked him up in the telephone directory.

After her second glass of wine, she called, apologized, and asked him over for sometime after ten, when Jeff would be asleep. By the time he arrived, she'd done the dishes, talked to Jeff for a while and picked up after him in the living room, even had time for a bath.

They talked about their children, then work, and then commiserated on the difficulties of being single at their age. Sometime after one o'clock, feeling less sleepy than she usually did at ten, Georgia asked Peter if he would like to go to bed with her. He said he would. Even though she felt at ease with him, she had a moment of regret that she hadn't taken the time to pick up a little bit in her room.

After they made love, she went out to the living room, barefoot across the icy floor, and brought back the wine and their glasses. She turned on the space heater she kept by her bed for reading late at night, and they lay in its warmth, talking together. Very domestic, she thought. She was propped on one elbow, with her body curved toward him. Looking down at him, and then herself, she noticed the flesh of her belly sagging onto the sheet in a gentle pouch. His eyes followed hers.

She stroked the curve of loose flesh. "Awful," she said.

"Hell," he said, "I'm not casting any first stones." He rested his hand on his balding head and smiled at her.

"I know," said Georgia. "But it's hard to get used to, isn't it?"

"What, getting old?"

"More just this new *body* that age brings you. To me, it still seems not mine. This body? Oh, I'm just wearing this for a while, while the old one . . ." She trailed off.

"Is at the cleaners."

"Something like that. And the old one was so nice. Ah, you should have known me then." She sipped her wine.

"I like knowing you now. I like the way you are now."

"You're kind."

"I'm lecherous."

"You're extraordinarily kind."

"You're crazy."

"I can't help it. I just feel so apologetic for what's here."

He laughed, and reached for her.

After a while, lying with her head resting on his chest, she said, "I've got an idea."

"What?"

"Just a second." She got up and went into the next room, her study. In the back of a file drawer, she found a small yellow cardboard box. She returned, carrying it to Peter.

"Wanna see?" she said. "Wanna see what a gorgeous chick I used to be?"

"What are these?"

She lay next to him on her stomach and lifted the first slide out of the box.

"My ex-husband took them of me when we were newlyweds. Homemade erotica, if there can be such a thing."

He held the slide toward the bedside lamp and squinted at a tiny body sleeping on a couch somewhere far away. Silently, she passed him the slides, one by one. He looked at each, and set it down in a small crooked pile on the white sheet. When he was done, he turned onto his back. After a moment he said, "Well, it's true. You did used to be younger."

Georgia felt shamed suddenly. She put the slides carefully back in the box, and set it on the bedside table.

"What time is it?" he asked.

"Almost three."

He sat up. "I'd better get going. I've got a squash game tomorrow at ten."

Georgia got up too, and put on her robe. She went into the living room and started to straighten up. She didn't want to watch him get ready to go.

She was waiting on the couch when he emerged from the bedroom, fully dressed. "You look elegant," she forced herself to say.

"I feel tired," he said.

She moved close to him at the door. He leaned over and kissed her quickly and, she thought, kindly.

"I'll call," he said. "Probably around the middle of the week."

After he'd gone, it took Georgia a long time to find some matches. She wasn't sure the slides would burn at all, but they did. She lit them one at a time in the bathroom sink and watched them changing into tiny hard pellets, like little droppings. Several times the flames illuminated a slide from underneath as it burned, and she could see clearly the tiny colored image of her own body years ago, languorous in the bathtub or sitting up in bed. It took almost an hour to burn them all. The smoke curled up black and chemical. It turned into delicate dark particles as it rose, and these descended slowly onto Georgia, like winter's first tentative snow.

# What Ernest Says

This is what Ernest whispers to her. "You ever had a man to go down on you? How you like me to be going down on you? How you like that? You like Ernest to eat you out?

"You ever suck black cock? How you like suckin me off?"

When Miss Foote calls on her, she is sometimes so confused that she just stares back. Her mouth hangs open, and she doesn't answer. The children laugh. They are glad to see her make a mistake. She is too smart, too big for her britches. Miss Foote calls her up after class. Why is she having so much trouble right now? Miss Foote used to be able to count on her. "You were someone I could rely on, Barbara, when I wanted an example for the other children."

Miss Foote's breath smells overripe, sweet, as though she had had cheese with her lunch several hours ago.

She doesn't look at Miss Foote. Just at her desk, the neat heaps of papers graded and stacked up. Barbara always gets S, superior, on her homework.

She tells Miss Foote she is sorry. She says no, she doesn't know what is wrong. Just sometimes now she has trouble concentrating in class. *Move me,* she wants to say, but she knows she mustn't ask to be moved away from the black kids. Her parents would be ashamed, so ashamed.

At recess the black kids gather under the viaduct. The white kids stay closer to the school. The white kids don't like the black kids. They say bad things about them. They call them *nigger, jigaboo.* Barbara's parents have told her they don't really feel these things, that they have learned them from their parents and don't know any better. Barbara's parents have told her the black kids are just as smart, just as good and nice as the white kids; they just need time and encouragement from the teachers to catch up. They say it is a shame that Miss Foote has all the black kids sitting together in the back of the room. They are glad Barbara is sitting next to them. They ask her if there is any one black child she talks to or has gotten to know.

Ernest, she tells them.

"Oh," her mother says brightly. "A boy. How interesting."

When Ernest leans forward, his breath is warm and sticky on Barbara's neck. She can feel her hairs stiffen in response, and a queer vibration passes down her spine, as though a part of that knotted bone had become, momentarily, gelatinous.

"I see you on Fifty-fifth this weekend, girl, and I call to you. You din answer me. You din hear me?"

She cannot even shake her head no. She wasn't on Fifty-fifth this weekend. She stayed home, except for Sunday, when she went to church, the church her parents belong to, where she is in a confirmation class. Though this church is in a neighborhood where many blacks live, very few of them come to the church. In Barbara's confirmation class, there are only white kids, three white girls, and Dr. Wilson, who has a tired face and a kind, hoarse voice. She stayed home all weekend except for church, and her mother said, "Isn't there somebody from school, some nice girl you'd like to have over?"

"The wind be blowin your skirt on Fifty-fifth, and I think I seen your pussy, girl. Is that right? Did you show me your pussy on Fifty-fifth? This was Saturday, I believe." His tone is so friendly, so conversational, that Barbara sometimes believes she makes up the words, the dirty words, in her own head. But how can she? She didn't know those words before he said them. She didn't know *cock, pussy, suck, eat.* Still she isn't sure what they mean, or if he really said them. Did he say them? Maybe he was saying something else. His accent, their accents are so thick sometimes she isn't sure what he says, what any of them say. When they talk together, she can understand almost nothing, but the girls' bright screams of laughter tell her it is all right, what they say to each other. Then it occurs to her, perhaps they are all laughing at her?

In class, Miss Foote asks a question. She calls on Sterling Cross. Barbara looks over at him, next to her. His face is blank. It is as though Miss Foote hadn't called on him. He blinks. The white kids have turned around to look at him. They wait. He scratches his head. His pale brown fingers make a soft noise Barbara can hear. Miss Foote calls on Ernest. Barbara's chair is attached to Ernest's desk. She feels it move slightly, but that is all. She knows how his face looks. Impassive, black; no one could expect an answer from it. The radiator hisses. To Barbara it seems that minutes have passed. Slowly she raises her hand. Miss Foote won't look at her. She is waiting for one of the black kids to answer. Barbara waves her hand.

Suddenly Miss Foote says in an irritated voice, "Barbara, you will have to learn you can't always be the center of attention."

Barbara is the smartest girl in class. There is one boy who is probably as smart as she is, Jimmy Nakagawa, but he won't talk when he is called on. He laughs to himself and shakes his head, so Miss Foote never calls on him at all anymore. Barbara and Jimmy Nakagawa never speak to each other, and hardly anyone else ever speaks to either of them. Barbara's parents' friends are always surprised when they hear where she goes to school. "She does just beautifully there," Barbara's mother says. "The instruction is really almost as good as in a private school, and we like her to meet all different kinds of children. She even has a special friend among the black children, a little boy named Ernest."

She is the smartest girl in confirmation class too. They are studying the sacraments, communion. Dr. Wilson says communion is the central ritual of Christian life. He reads Christ's words: "Take, eat, this is my Body, which is given for you; do this in remembrance of me." He asks the girls what the sacrament of communion means. No one raises a hand or says anything. He looks at Barbara. Barbara has studied this. She knows the answer, but she cannot remember it. The room is silent. Dr. Wilson looks angry and tired. He begins to answer his own question. The next Sunday, Barbara is sick and doesn't have to go to church or confirmation class. She stays in the house all weekend.

"Hey, girl. I be waitin for you last Saturday. You told me you meet me under the viaduck and I wait for you maybe three hours." Barbara shakes her head in confusion. "Why you tell me that when you not goin to meet me, why you do that?"

She never looks at Ernest when he talks to her, but she knows how he looks, she can imagine his mouth as she feels his humid whisper. It is as pink as bubble gum inside, his tongue is pink too, his lips slowly turn pink as they curve into his warm mouth.

Sometimes at recess Barbara stands near the viaduct and listens to the black kids. There are three girls who sing together—Norma Jean is one of them—and Barbara likes the way their voices move so close. Their voices almost touch each other but don't. "Red hots, french fries," they sing, and clap. "And chili macs." Ernest is smoking a cigarette. He sees her looking at him and says something to James. They laugh.

Barbara tells her father she doesn't want to be confirmed. She doesn't feel ready to take communion, to drink the blood, to eat the body of Christ. Her father is understanding. She will go to church with them on Sunday still but not be confirmed, and, for now, stop the confirmation classes. "What's most important," he says to Barbara, "is to listen to your own inner voice."

Sometimes he doesn't speak to her for days. Behind her back, she hears him talking, laughing, with James, with Sterling, with

Norma Jean. She waits for the pause, the break, then the softer, moist voice near her head. She listens to the silence behind her when Miss Foote is talking. She stares intently at Miss Foote's moving mouth, the gold teeth in the back flashing occasionally. She listens to Ernest's breath behind her. Miss Foote calls on her and she stares and doesn't answer.

Miss Foote is upset and sends for her mother. Her mother is concerned. Perhaps there is some physiological problem. Barbara goes to the eye doctor, the ear doctor. The ear doctor whispers at the back of her head, "Can you hear this?" His breath is cool, but it stirs the hairs on her neck. "Yes. Yes," she whispers back with her eyes closed, like a lover in the dark. There is nothing wrong with her, they say. It's nothing organic.

Ernest's desk is empty. Barbara leans back in her chair and watches the door as the latecomers straggle in. After the Pledge of Allegiance, Miss Foote calls the roll and then talks about Ernest. His sixteenth birthday was the day before and he won't be back. Miss Foote says this is a tragedy, that Ernest should have tried to finish eighth grade anyway, that people should always try to finish what they have begun. She talks about how Ernest is hurting his chances forever to be a success, to make something of himself, by quitting now. She hopes everyone in this classroom will finish eighth grade, whatever their age, whatever their background or skin color, and think about high school, and even college.

In her seat, Barbara tries to hide the slow tears starting down her face.

# Travel

The room at the tourist hotel was small, with casement windows that opened out over the kitchen annex. Starting at about seven in the morning, the happy incomprehensible banter of the kitchen staff, the crash and clatter of garbage cans and dishes, would rise into Oley and Rob's room. Oley lay in bed and listened. From the bathroom floated in the smell of fermenting strawberries. Oley and Rob had bought them at the market on their first day in Trujillo. An impassive Indian woman had sat next to an enormous basket of the fruit, a deep basket at least four feet in diameter. It seemed romantic, the luxuriance of so many strawberries gleaming uniformly fat and red, so unlike the parsimony of pint boxes in the supermarket at home, boxes in which only the top layer of fruit was red; the buyer knew that distributed underneath were the ones with hard white patches or soft sides. Oley and Rob bought a large bag of the fruit from the Indian woman, and a bottle of wine. On their first night in the hotel they'd played gin rummy in their room, eating and drinking. Then, drunk, full, they'd made love, smelling the strawberries in each other's mouths, and then on each other's skin, everywhere.

Rob was gone from the bed already. Probably out taking pictures. He was doing a travel article. It had been gray and overcast since they'd arrived in Trujillo, so he didn't want to do the ruins yet, or the plaza. He got up early to do interiors—churches, museums—before they were crowded with people, whose appeal or lack of it to potential tourists he couldn't control. Once she would have gone with him, held the cameras and lenses he wasn't using. But there was some silent agreement they'd reached about this now and he let her sleep on alone.

She got up and went into the bathroom. The smell of fermenting strawberries was much stronger, almost sickening, in here. The plastic bag rested on the windowsill, and she could see that the strawberries had exuded a little pool of pinkish liquid, in which they sat. She picked up the bag and dropped it into the wastebasket. A little of it had oozed out onto the sill.

As she hunched over on the toilet, the complicated, funky smell of their lovemaking the night before rose to her nostrils too. She reached over to the sink and filled the water glass. She lowered it between her legs and splashed herself with little handfuls of the warm water four or five times. She stood up and dabbed at herself with a towel. Bright laughter floated up from the kitchen. She pushed the heavy nickel handle and the toilet flushed violently.

Rob came back full of energy, with presents for Oley. He dumped them on her naked thighs as she lay stretched out on the bed, and then sat in the room's only chair, the desk chair, to watch her open them. There was a little white box that held silver earrings and a necklace nested in slightly soiled cotton; a tiny, brightly colored basket in a brown paper bag; and a greenish fruit he couldn't remember the name of. She thanked him over and over. She put on the jewelry and looked at herself in the hand mirror he gave her. The dangling earrings brushed against the sides of her neck.

"And pictures?" she asked. She was trying to be generous too. "Did you get any good pictures?"

He raised the camera, as though to fiddle with it. Then it was in front of his face. It clicked. "One, anyway," he said, and smiled at her.

Olympia had flown to Lima with money that Rob had mailed to her. He'd called her long-distance three times from Peru before she'd agreed to join him. She had at first been determined not to. Rob had decided only two months earlier that he couldn't marry her. They'd been living together for more than a year. She had asked him to move out.

He wanted her to join him, he said on the phone, because he was lonely, because they'd always traveled so well together. Why couldn't they still be loving friends, especially in a faraway place? She ought to see Peru at least this once. He'd be more than happy to pay all her expenses.

Oley had missed Rob, the excitement he brought into her life. She'd grown up in a safe, small town and was a little afraid of anything new or random. In New Haven she was a teacher; her work was regular and held no surprises for her. When Rob had lived with her, was her lover, she liked the feeling of involvement with passing events he introduced her to, the way life seemed to reach in and touch him. His voice on the telephone seemed like that exciting, random touch. She decided to go.

After she'd made the decision, when she began to think about seeing Rob again, Oley felt, in spite of herself, a return of the hope that had fueled her during their year together: the hope that given enough time, she could will Rob into the kind of love that would make him want to stay. She had to consciously remind herself that she was going only to have a good time, only to travel.

And at first it had seemed as though it might work on that basis. In the airport, watching him walk toward her, tanned, his hair longer than when she'd last seen him, she felt a rush of intense passion that made her throat hurt. They'd had the night with the strawberries and for a few days after that they'd been happy. Rob made little ceremonies of every meal, every gift he gave her. She spoke no Spanish and so he had to act as her interpreter to the world. She felt sheltered and protected, cared for in a way that hadn't been possible for a long time at home. There her toughness, her competence, had been things she felt she needed to stress as it became clearer and clearer to her that he was choosing not to marry her.

But as the slow days passed in Trujillo, Oley came to resent the very gifts, the courtliness that had at first charmed her. She was sometimes unpleasant to Rob, petulant. She didn't like herself then, but she wasn't able to stop. Everything he gave her, everything he did for her, reminded her only of what he wouldn't give, wouldn't do.

As they crossed the plaza on their way to the bakery, three little boys with shoeshine kits followed them, their clothes ragged, their faces dirty. They were always on the plaza, noisy and cheerful. The first day, Rob and Oley had decided to have a shoeshine, and had hired the two thinnest, smallest boys. A group of ten or so, all with their wooden kits, assembled to watch the process, chatting and commenting while the chosen boys stylishly and elaborately polished and buffed. On the final buffing, their cloths took on a life of their own, cracking and whipping through the air.

The second day, in their eagerness for business, the boys had followed Rob and Oley without noticing that they were both wearing sandals. Rob had stopped finally and pointed this out. He'd asked them what color they would polish his bare feet, and they'd laughed at this joke, at themselves. Now they always trailed behind Rob and Oley, laughing, calling out. They seemed to like Rob. He told Oley that they'd become very familiar, were sometimes quite insulting in their comments on the condition of his Frye boots, of Oley's shoes.

Today Rob delivered a long dramatic monologue to the boys as they crossed the plaza, his face and voice mournful. The boys laughed and danced around him, egging him on. Oley felt edged out, ignored.

They crossed to a side street, leaving the ragged group behind, and Oley asked him what he'd been saying.

"Long sad story," said Rob. He lifted an imaginary violin and began to play. "I'm so poor I can't afford even a shoeshine. And if I had the money I ought to take it home to my even poorer mother, who sits alone with fourteen babies, trying to make supper from a cup of meal and one starving guinea pig. In fact, if I had the money, I ought to take it home to the guinea pig of my mother, who hasn't had anything to eat since . . ." He stopped abruptly, looking at Oley.

"Not funny, O?" He bent to look at her face. "You no like?"

She shook her head. They walked a block in silence. The dark men turned to stare at Oley, who was tall and fair, with straight blond hair hanging down her back and over her shoulders.

"Well, I'd hate to ask you *why,*" Rob said finally, with hostility in his voice. "I'd be so fucking scared you'd tell me."

She pressed her lips together, and then spoke. She'd never felt more like a schoolteacher. "It seems unkind," she said, "when by their standards we're so rich, for you to make fun of their poverty."

He shrugged. "Therein, of course, lies the joke," he said. They turned into the bakery, pushing aside the beaded curtain. Everyone looked up at them for a moment, at the tall, long-haired man dressed a little like a cowboy in his jeans and work shirt, and his blond companion. "Clearly they thought it was funny," he said, behind her. "If they can laugh at it, then there must be some level on which it *is* funny."

There were empty tables in the back, and they walked toward them through the groups of Peruvians nearer the front. There were mostly men in the bakery, except for the women who worked behind the counter.

"The trouble with you, Oley, is that you always imagine everyone else has exactly your sensibility." As he said this, Rob was pulling the chair out for Oley. She sat down. "And they don't. They don't. By and large, the human race is tougher and has a better sense of humor than you do, O."

He sat down opposite her and Oley looked at him. She would never, she felt, not find him attractive.

"That's just how *you* imagine them," she said. "And that's just because you think everyone is like *you*. So you see, we're not really so different after all."

Oley had met Rob when he came to take photographs of the preschool kids she taught. Oley, who was often somber and shy when she met new people, whose high school yearbook photo had "Still Waters Run Deep" under it, was animated and energetic around the children. Rob took as many pictures of her as he did of the kids.

She was aware of using her playfulness with the children to charm him, and felt, a few times during the day, guilty enough about this element of duplicity to draw back suddenly into a shy stiffness. But the children insisted on the Oley they knew. "Not *that* way, Oley," they'd say. "Do it the *other* way, the *silly* way."

He took her out for dinner that night. The combination of his own almost childish energy and his having seen her earlier so full of life made it easier for her to continue what she couldn't help thinking of as a charade during the meal. Even as they made love back in her apartment, she wanted to tell him he'd made a mistake, that she wasn't who he thought she was.

As the week in Trujillo went by, Oley and Rob spent more and more time after dinner in the hotel bar. They played gin rummy, keeping a running score, and drank foaming, lemony Pisco sours. The bar was as old as the rest of the hotel, paneled in mahogany and mirrored on one side. Louvered doors opened into the dining room and the lobby. A large fan with wooden blades twirled slowly overhead. The bartender, a short, plump Indian man with liquid black eyes, stared at Oley almost constantly; at her size, they speculated, at her blondness, her freckles.

"And my boobs," Oley said. She was drunk. "Boobs'll do it every time, the world over. It's amazing how predictable it all is."

"I'll drink to that. I'll drink to predictability," he said, spreading his cards on the table, "and I'll go down with three."

"Bastard," she said.

They still made love every night, always with the same skillful familiarity with each other's bodies, but they postponed until later and later the time when they'd leave the warm light of the bar and climb the wide wooden staircase together. Each night, undressing, getting ready for sure pleasure, Oley felt increasingly that it was a capitulation that shamed her somehow. More than once they were the last people to leave the bar, but the solemn, handsome bartender never complained, never rushed them, never stopped staring and blushing.

"He loves you, O," Rob said. He lay naked on the bed, watching Oley undress.

"I know," Oley said sadly. She carefully folded her jeans and shirt, then came to sit on the edge of the bed.

"You know how I know?" Rob asked.

"No."

" 'Cause he doesn't charge us for about half of what we drink. Your half, I figure." He had moved over to accommodate her. Now he began to stroke her back and arms.

Oley looked at him. "Is that true?"

"As sure as I'm about to screw you madly."

"No, wait. Tell me the truth." She put her hands on his, to still them. "He's been giving us free drinks?"

"Yes. *You,* anyway. I asked that Chilean guy, you know, the one with the fat wife and all the kids?" Oley nodded. "I asked him if he was getting free drinks and he said not. Said it must be because the guy's so smitten with you. *Everybody* knows it, Oley. My big, blond Oley."

She turned from him. "Oh, that's so sad."

"Why? What's so sad about it?"

"I don't know. Everything. That he's a grown man; and his world is so small that he sees me as some kind of *princess.* And all he has to offer me is Pisco sours. And I'm up here fucking you, who couldn't care less at some level. And he ends up, really, giving *you* the drinks. It just all seems so . . . misplaced and pathetic."

Rob was silent a moment. Then he began stroking her arm again. His hand touched lightly the side of Oley's breast and she felt the dropping sensation inside that was, for her, the beginning of desire. "Well, he can't give you the drinks without treating me too. That's just how it is."

"I know. That's what I mean."

They sat in silence. Then Rob said, "I *do* care, O. I can't do it your way, but I do care."

"I know," she said. And then, because she was very drunk, she said again, "That's what I mean."

Oley had thought she wouldn't hear from Rob again after their first night together. She had gotten used to this in New Haven, though it was something she'd been unprepared for when she first arrived—that men could sleep with you and then simply never call you, never try to see you again. She had had one lover all through college, actually someone she'd known a little in high school too, so her experience was limited. And such a thing would have been in some sense impossible in the town where she'd grown up, if only because she would have known the man, or at least who he was, before she slept with him, and would have continued to see him at least occasionally afterward. In New Haven, men could just disappear, and did; although she would occasionally glimpse someone she'd slept with going into a bookstore or crossing a street. A few times she'd waved or said hello, but she realized by their lack of response that she wasn't supposed to do that. She wasn't supposed to exist anymore; she was just a place they'd been, a town they'd passed through and chosen not to visit again.

After the painful shock of the first few times, that was all right with Oley. It gave her a kind of freedom she hadn't imagined possible, and she discovered a side to herself sexually that was different and wilder than any of the parts of herself that lived responsibly day by day in New Haven.

Besides, she had come to understand that the men who would call her back were people she thought of as thick, dull; people who saw only the good, steady side of herself. The men she liked, the men who let her imagine herself as other than the way she was, were not men who wanted to spend much time with quiet young Head Start teachers.

And so, when Rob called back, she was surprised and even a little disturbed. There was a part of her that didn't want to have to cope with him as a real possibility, as a real disappointment. But she told him she'd meet him for a drink Friday evening to look at the proofs of the pictures he'd taken; and when she saw them, she saw suddenly who she could be, how she could be, with him. Off and on during the difficult year he'd lived with her, Oley would look at the pictures he'd taken of her before he knew who she was, in order to remind herself of what she could be to someone else.

Rob left Oley alone in the hotel for two days. A reporter they'd met who was covering the revolutionary movement for a British paper had told him that the rebels were planning to take over the train from Cuzco to Machu Picchu. Rob thought he should fly in right away and get his pictures. He didn't think it was a good idea for Oley to come along. It was as he stood peeling bills from a roll of money he carried with him that Oley understood how completely dependent on him she'd let herself become in this world. She was actually frightened to be alone.

The first day she didn't deviate from the routines they had set up together. Wherever she went, she smiled and nodded at the people who spoke to her. Laboriously she counted out money when she made a purchase, and occasionally she murmured the Spanish Rob had taught her for "I don't understand" when someone seemed to expect her to respond. Otherwise she was silent and alone all day. In the evening she ate in the hotel dining room and went to bed early, without stopping in the bar.

But the next morning the sun was shining for the first time since Oley had arrived in Peru, and after breakfast she went to the desk in the hotel lobby and asked the clerk about transportation to the ruins.

"Ah, the Professor!" the clerk said, and made a quick phone call. Then she explained to Oley that there was a local expert on the ruins who would take her on a guided tour for free, a kind of promotional deal he offered. He would come for her in his car later in the afternoon.

He showed up at about three-thirty. Oley was surprised at his appearance. He looked like a Latin crooner, a slicked-back Andy Williams. He wore pale clothes and a golfer's sweater, buttoned casually at the waist. His mustache was thin, his hair a preposterously brilliant black, and he spoke careful, formal English. He smiled at Oley and revealed elaborate structures of gold where most of his teeth should have been.

When Oley went outside with him, she discovered that his car was an ornately finned American model from the fifties, badly repainted a bilious green. There were several other passengers in it, other distinguished visitors to Peru, the Professor told Oley. The car had been fitted with a broken plastic cap on its roof, which now read TAX. Oley hesitated a moment, then inquired whether she could not pay the Professor something for the privilege of taking the tour with him. The Professor assured her that it was his privilege, he was pleased to do it *gratis,* in order to let people know about his shop, a shop specializing in reproductions of the ruins' artifacts.

As Oley got in, the Professor introduced the other tourists. The Indian man behind the wheel revved the car noisily, and they sped away from the tourist hotel, leaving a trail of rubber and exhaust to delight the shoeshine boys gathered on the plaza.

The car had no shocks at all, and on every bump and curve, Oley and the other passengers were thrown and swung from side to side in the back seat. The Professor sat in front with a massive Dutch woman, who had, like him, a small mustache. He rested his arm along the back of the seat, and with his face turned to his group, he made conversation in his stilted English about the ruins, about their countries of origin, about Peru.

Oley, glad to have an opportunity to speak English at last, grew expansive. She chatted with the massive Dutch woman and her shy female companion, and with the skinny and uncommunicative German student who completed their group.

It took about fifteen minutes to get to the ruins. They loomed ugly and unpromising in the flat terrain, so many dirt piles. Up close, more of what they might once have been was visible, and there were groups of archaeology students working to restore them; but Oley was disappointed. She was in the process of deciding that she preferred the living, slightly decrepit town to the parched desolation of the ruins, when they came to the sections where intact samples of the relief work remained in the sand. Abruptly her disappointment vanished. The artwork here was both stylized and sexual, and Oley found herself moved by it. But the Professor's explanations of the meaning of the figures irritated her. He kept talking about things like the symbolic fusion of the spirit and the will as he stood in front of the intertwined tongues and bodies. The Dutch woman, her friend and the German student stood, listened, nodded. But Oley began to lag behind the group. The Professor frowned at her, calling out from time to time that she was missing the discussion of the detail. Momentarily she would rejoin them; but then she would again find his monologue maddening, and drop back. She felt as though she were a naughty American child among adults.

On their way back to town, the driver pulled off the highway into what looked like an abandoned gas station. It was the Professor's gallery. The group of gringos clambered obediently out of the car, which rose several inches with each one's departure. The shop was sweltering. It was full of black-and-white prints, scrolls and little clay sculptures. The Professor swung into a sales pitch. He had a way of unrolling the prints that reminded Oley of the shoeshine boys, their elaborate display with their cloths.

The Dutch woman seemed interested. After looking at what seemed to Oley an endless number of samples, she bought two prints. Oley had moved nearer to the door, waiting for the transactions to be over. The reproductions in the shop were stark, precise, Egyptian. They had none of the sensuality of the actual reliefs, and they seemed expensive to Oley. And even though there were a few less expensive, less unattractive pieces of sculpture, Oley didn't want anything. The moment the Professor had gone into his pitch, she felt angry at him for trapping her here, for his false generosity. She was determined to buy nothing.

The German student liked one of the prints, but said that the price was too high. Oley moved into the doorway to try to catch a breeze as she watched the Professor at work. He came down a bit; the student, more animated than he'd been all day, pushed for an even lower price. Slowly they narrowed in on the range they could agree on, and the purchase was made. Then the little group was left standing in the shop, waiting for a signal from the Professor that they could leave, that his driver would take them back. But it became clear that he, in turn, was waiting for Oley to buy something. Everyone else had paid the price for the tour. It was her turn. The group looked expectantly at her.

The Professor walked over closer to her and picked up one of the clay figures. "You have, perhaps, found something you would like, Miss Erickson?" he asked.

"No. Nothing," Oley answered. She could hear the defiance in her own voice.

The Professor paused for only a moment. "Ah, well, then," he said. "Perhaps I can point out to you some things which you may not have noticed." He gestured to where the scrolls lay rolled up like tubes of wallpaper on the shelf.

There was another moment of silence. Then Oley, still standing in the doorway, said, "I'm not going to buy anything, Professor. I'm sorry, I misunderstood your meaning, and really thought the tour was free." Oley thought she could feel the group recoil from her slightly in the shop. "Besides," she said, "I really can't afford it."

She turned and walked outside, let herself into the car. The driver, leaning against the auto in the hot sun, looked confused. Slowly the little group of tourists meandered out too. Last came the Professor, looking seedy and defeated. Oley felt sorry for him, actually. The driver took his silent lurching load back to town.

When Oley got back to the tourist hotel, she went up to her room. She ran herself a deep tub and lay in it for a long while, occasionally twisting the old-fashioned nickel-plated knob with her toes to let more hot water in. Her breasts floated above the water. The nipples tightened in the cool air. Oley dipped a washcloth into the steaming tub and laid it across her chest.

She lay in the tub until the sky outside turned purple; then black. When she got out, her fingers and toes were wrinkled into what she and her mother had called "raisin skin" when she was small. She noticed, on the windowsill, a little red stain the maid had missed when she cleaned, the hardened juice of the strawberries.

She dressed and went to the bar. She sat at one of the wooden tables by herself and ordered a Pisco sour. The table was next to the louvered windows which opened out onto the plaza. Through the slats she could see, in the glare of the fluorescent streetlamps, the shoeshine boys, their workday over, huddled in a tiny group around one bench. She watched them.

From time to time during the evening, one of the other guests with whom she was familiar—the fat wife of the Chilean, the British reporter—came and talked to Oley for a while. But for the most part she sat alone. The bartender brought over a fresh drink or bowl of peanuts as soon as she'd finished the one before. Slowly the boys on the plaza drifted away. When the last two lay down on one of the benches, Oley got up. She bumped into a chair on her way to the bar, and its legs scraped noisily on the bare floor.

She asked the bartender how much everything was. He looked at her, his eyes blazing with devotion, and shook his head. "Please," she said in Spanish, "how much?" Again he shook his head. Oley felt her eyes fill with tears. "You are very generous," she said in English. "Too generous." He smiled shyly, partly, Oley saw, because he was missing several teeth. "Thank you," he said in slow English. She reached over and touched the immaculate sleeve of his white coat. "No," she said. "Thank *you*. Gracias. Thank you." She patted his arm gently; then turned and carefully walked out of the bar.

Rob came back early the next morning. Oley was still in bed, a little hung over. Rob was excited. He had met a man on the plane from Cuzco who wanted to buy American dollars and would meet him on the plaza in half an hour. Oley got out of bed and dressed slowly. Rob paced the room impatiently, leaned out the casement window into the kitchen noise. Oley knew it wasn't just the illegal exchange rate that excited him, but the idea of the black market, of doing something illicit. She was familiar with this impulse of his. He'd once, for the same reason, bought a gun from a black guy they'd met at a bar in New Haven. He didn't want it for anything. He had kept it for months in the bureau drawer in her apartment.

He and Oley had made a special trip to Block Island by ferry in order to get rid of it, finally. They hadn't even stayed overnight. They just took the ferry over, dropping the gun in the water on the way, and returned that evening.

As they stepped out of the hotel lobby, Oley looked over toward the plaza. The sky was white again today, with high clouds. The flat gray stones in the plaza still gleamed darkly from their daily early-morning washing. The shoeshine boys, six or seven of them today, stood near the fountain at the plaza's center, talking and gesturing. Two of the cement benches that studded the radiating pathways of the plaza were occupied, one by an itinerant secretary, the typewriter on his knees clattering faintly in the morning air as the old man next to him dictated, the other by a man in a sports jacket and sunglasses, holding a briefcase on his lap.

"Is that the guy?" Olympia asked.

"The very one," Rob said. He patted his shirt pocket. Before they'd left their room, he'd put eight hundred-dollar bills into it, folded in half. Oley had protested that it seemed too much, but he'd said they would need it in Arequipa, the next city on their itinerary.

The shoeshine boys spotted Rob and approached, waving and calling out. Even though Rob barely nodded to them, they followed him and Oley over to the man. But when Rob and Oley sat down and began talking, they fell back slightly. A few of them set their kits down and sat on them at a little distance, watching the trio on the bench.

The man chatted politely with Oley and Rob for a while, at first about how they liked traveling in Peru. Their enthusiasm seemed to amuse him. He was slim and good-looking. His face was slightly pockmarked. He began to talk about himself. He seemed anxious to explain himself to Oley in particular. He spoke fluent English, with only a slight accent. He'd gone to school in America, UCLA, he told Oley, and majored in engineering. He wanted to leave Peru, where his opportunities were so limited, to move to the United States; but the government wouldn't let him take Peruvian money out of the country. "They would strip me of my birthright, as it were," he said. "My parents are not wealthy, but they have worked hard all of their lives for me, for their only son. But the government would have me leave the country a pauper. You, a rich North American, must understand that I cannot go to the United States a pauper."

"I'm not rich," said Oley.

"Of course you are," said the man politely.

"No." Oley shook her head. "Really. I'm a schoolteacher. Schoolteachers aren't rich."

"Schoolteachers in America are rich," the man announced in his gentle, apologetic voice. "They own houses, cars, land."

Oley thought of her tiny apartment on the fringe of the ghetto in New Haven. She felt, suddenly, a pang of homesickness for its bare familiarity. She wanted to describe it to the man, but she knew there was no point.

"And here I find you traveling in my country," he persisted gently. "Such travel is expensive, is it not?"

Rob was watching Oley with interest. Oley saw that he expected her to say that the money was his, to separate herself from him, repudiate him, as she'd done in one way or another, she realized, all week. She felt suddenly as though she should apologize to him.

"Yes, you're right," she said to the man. Her voice was soft and regretful, as though she were acknowledging something shameful about herself. "It is terribly expensive."

She felt Rob's eyes on her.

"Well, then," the man said. "You understand my circumstance entirely, then. Americans don't like poor foreigners, so that I must be certain, before I leave, to amass enough money to fit easily and smoothly into your world."

He turned to Rob and they proceeded to the details of their exchange. Oley watched them. Rob's face was animated, lively, full of the energy that had always attracted her, that she had always wanted to have herself, but didn't. He and the man laughed about something. Oley looked over at the shoeshine boys. She felt like them, shut out, an onlooker.

The man opened the briefcase on his knees. He left the lid up to shield the interior from view, but the shoeshine boys had caught a glimpse of its contents. They seemed in unison, audibly, to draw their breath in.. They approached slightly nearer and made a silent semicircle around the three adults on the bench. In the briefcase, neatly banded, were stacks of Peruvian currency, perhaps more than most of the shoeshine boys would earn in a lifetime. They watched with rapt attention, whispering a little among themselves, as Rob and the man exchanged dollars for soles. Oley noted that when she and Rob got up and walked away, the shoeshine boys for the first time didn't follow or call to them. Unmolested, she and Rob walked back into the cool, dim lobby of the tourist hotel.

When they got up to their room, Rob began pulling the money from his pockets and throwing it on the bed. "We're rich, Oley! Rich! Rich!" he cried. Oley sat in the chair and watched him. When he'd emptied his pockets and turned to her, grinning, she said softly, "I've got to go home, Rob." He looked at her for a moment, the smile fading, and then he sat down on the bed without pushing the money out of the way.

"Oley," he said. He shook his head. "Olympia. How come I knew you were going to say that?"

In late August, Oley found a manila envelope leaning against the door to her apartment. It was postmarked New York and stamped PHOTOGRAPH. DO NOT BEND. Because it was very hot outside and she'd been at a faculty meeting all day, she went around the apartment throwing open the windows and then she fixed herself a glass of iced tea before she opened it. Inside was a blowup of the picture Rob had taken of her in the tourist hotel in Trujillo. Oley felt in the corners of the envelope for a written message, but there was none. Just the picture. She looked at it carefully.

Wearing the delicate necklace and earrings that she still had in the dresser in her bedroom, the Oley in the picture stretched out naked on the bed and looked directly into the camera. Rob had lightened her body and darkened the background, so she seemed almost to float toward the camera, her gaze blankened and bold.

Oley looked at the picture a long time, trying to recognize herself in it. Then she picked up her iced tea and carried it into the bedroom. The cubes clinked gently together as she walked. She set the glass down on top of the bureau, opened the top drawer, and took out the necklace and earrings. Standing in front of her full-length mirror, she took off all her clothes and put on the jewelry. She looked at her familiar reflection—the solid wide hips, the large breasts, the pubic hair dark in spite of her blondness. She stood in her bedroom and looked at herself. On the breeze that stirred through the apartment and lightly touched her body floated the sound of someone's transistor radio, the rhythm of teenaged voices in conversation. She closed her eyes and tried to imagine herself making love with Rob, the familiar sequence of sensations she had thought of as shapes they made together. She couldn't. That possibility seemed remote, as far away as the small town she'd grown up in, as far away as the Olympia Rob had created in the photograph.

# Leaving Home

"Go find Daddy," Anita said in the kitchen. "Where did Daddy go?"

Leah was in the closet in the living room, and Anita's voice sounded muted and thickened to her. The closet smelled of mildew and camphor, and was full of old boots and boxes of clothing. Leah knelt among them and listened to Anita cross from the kitchen to the foot of the stairs.

"The baby stinks, Greg." Anita's voice was closer, sharper. There was silence from upstairs.

"Did you hear me, Greg? The baby stinks and it's my birthday. I'm not going to change her." Anita walked back to the kitchen, past Sophie, who had followed her across the living room. Leah rose and stepped out of the closet to watch her grandchild. The little girl had just learned to walk and she held her amazed hands up in the air and waved them for balance with each exaggerated step, a miniature tightrope walker. There was a large wet stain down one leg of her overalls.

Greg lumbered down the stairs, and Sophie smiled up at him. Her bare feet curved inward at the toe. Greg squatted in front of her. "Soph, you did it again," he said. Then he noticed his mother, standing in the closet doorway. "Isn't that something?" he asked her, as though Sophie had just performed some prodigious musical or artistic feat. His face was deadpan.

Leah laughed, pushing her curly hair off her face.

"Do you stink, Soph?" he asked the child. "Are you, in fact, a . . . *stinker?*"

Sophie smiled, watching him with delight.

"Are you"—he paused again, and in anticipation she made a small squealing noise—"a *stinker?*" She laughed and set her tiny hands on his face.

"Are you"—she had the game now, and was already laughing, but watched him rapturously until he had said it—"a *stinker?*" Her body gave itself up to laughter, and she suddenly lost her balance and sat down hard on the floor, still laughing.

"Look how smart she is, honey," Leah said. "She just picks up anything so fast."

"If she's so smart, how come she isn't toilet trained?" He scooped her up and held her balanced horizontally across his hip. A strand of drool dangled from her mouth and was suddenly gone, a drop on the floor. Sophie watched it, fascinated.

"What were you doing in the closet, Mom?" Greg asked.

"Trying to find the damn picnic basket."

"Didn't you used to keep it in the basement?"

"Yes, but we had a picnic just a week or so ago, and I thought I put it away up here."

He stood looking at his mother for a moment. She was still pretty, in a slightly plump, worn way. She was wearing jeans and an old T-shirt that had his high school emblem on it.

"Who is this 'we' that keeps cropping up?"

Leah blushed. "Just a man I've been seeing a little of."

"Just a man?"

She nodded.

"Wasn't there a movie called *Just a Man?*" He shifted Sophie on his hip.

"No," Leah said. "You're thinking of *Nothing But a Man.*"

"No I'm not, Mom. I'm thinking of this movie *Just a Man.* It's different from *Nothing But a Man.*"

"God, that was a good movie, that *Nothing But a Man.*" Leah's hand strayed to her hair again. "And the sound track. I mean, it wasn't a musical, but do you remember that song 'Heat Wave'?"

"No, but you do." Sophie began to make complaining noises, and wriggled. "Okay, Soph, here we go," he said.

"I can't believe it," Leah said, as he turned to go up the stairs. "You don't remember 'Heat Wave.' "

He laughed. "That was your life, Mom."

Leah stood a moment at the bottom of the stairs and watched him carry Sophie up, jouncing her on each step. "Hup, hup," he said. Then she turned and crossed to the kitchen.

The kitchen was flooded with early-afternoon sunlight. Anita sat at the round wooden table by the windows, drinking coffee and reading the paper. The lunch dishes still littered the table. Anita had said she would do them. Leah had to will herself not to start cleaning up.

She sat down at what had been her place and sipped at the cold milky coffee left in her cup.

Anita lowered the paper. She was wearing her glasses, two clear, thick circles with steel-rimmed frames that perched weightlessly on her perfect nose. She was a law student. Most of the time Leah had trouble imagining her, delicate and frail as she seemed, in that competitive world. But now, wearing her glasses, she looked icy and determined. Leah didn't know if Greg had married Anita for her eggshell-frail beauty or for the steely competence that lay underneath it. Or both, of course. When he told her they were getting married, she asked him why. He seemed too young to Leah, hopelessly young. "Because, Mom," he answered earnestly then, "she's someone I know I can live with the rest of my life." She was touched by his conviction and ashamed of the impulse she had to mock him for it. Now she looked at Anita. Why can't I ever tell what she's thinking? Leah wondered. Why does she make me feel like the younger of us two. She sighed.

"What's up?" Anita asked.

"Oh, just nothing's working today, and now I can't find the damned picnic basket."

"What's it look like?"

Leah instantly felt annoyed. She didn't want Anita's help. She didn't want Anita to find it for her.

"The way they look. A big square hampery kind of thing."

"Oh. I might have seen it, I think."

"Where?"

"The broom closet by the back door, maybe?"

Leah went to the broom closet and opened the door. The hamper sat on the top shelf, beyond her easy reach. Joe, so much taller, so much more domestic than she, must have put it away after their picnic. She stood on her toes and, with the tips of her fingers, slid the basket forward on the shelf until it leaned suddenly toward her and she caught it. She had thought about asking him over tonight. It was Anita's birthday, her twenty-fifth, and they were going to have a party outside in the backyard. Greg had invited Pete Slattery, his closest friend from high school, and his wife. She and Joe had talked about whether he should come, but they had decided no. Two of his children still lived at home, and when Leah and Joe were together at his house they felt obliged to adopt a pose of almost marital stability. They both liked the sense of freedom, of abandon, they had at her house. Last Sunday after breakfast, they had made love in the kitchen. Leah had sat in the bright summer light on the counter amid the egg-stained dishes and chipped coffee mugs, the sun warming her back and Joe warming her front; and she had cried out, "Oh. Oh. Oh," as loudly as she wanted when she came. After all her years of negotiated privacy when Greg was young, of sneaking the occasional lover in and out of the house, as though she were the teenager, and Greg—heavily asleep in his room, which smelled of dirty socks and the sulfurous acne medication he wore to bed—

were the parent, she was jealous of her long-awaited freedom, her claim to sexuality. They decided there was no rush for Joe to meet her family.

But a few hours before Anita and Greg were to arrive, he'd turned up at her back door with a present, a loaf of zucchini bread he'd made for the party. It was wrapped in aluminum foil, and it was still warm in Leah's hands as she stood with him on the back stoop.

"It smells good. Is it supposed to be your version of a silver bullet, Joe? Who was that masked man, and all that?"

She blocked the kitchen doorway. She was embarrassed for Joe to see how much neater the house was than usual. Even though he stood several steps below her, Joe's head was level with hers.

"It's supposed to make you remember me. You're going to eat a piece of that bread and want me in the middle of the family doings."

She held the present against her. The heat touched her breasts through her shirt. "If I had to pick something to remind you of me in my absence, it wouldn't be zucchini bread," she said, after a moment.

He shrugged and grinned at her. He was a skinny man, balding, with one eye that swiveled out as though to check on what was going on in the rest of the world. She had told him that she'd never have been attracted to him if it weren't for the wild freedom of that eye. She had felt a positive erotic charge trying to meet his difficult gaze when they'd been introduced, at a parent-teacher night in the high school, where his youngest child, a girl named Fiona, was Leah's student. "Well," he said, "actually we just had too goddamn many zucchini in the garden. That's the bald-faced truth of the situation."

"Oh, don't tell me the bald-faced truth," she said. "I never want to hear that." He kept grinning as he leaned forward to kiss her. His tongue came a little way into her mouth. Then he was gone, gone until this weekend of her being a mother again was over.

Now, as Leah brought the hamper over to the kitchen table, Anita got up lazily and started to carry the lunch dishes to the sink. What had bothered her most about the scene at the foot of the stairs, Leah suddenly thought, watching her tall daughter-in-law move across the kitchen, graceful as a giraffe, was that Anita had called Sophie "the baby." She ought to say her name.

Around three o'clock, with the house in a dazed silence because of the heat and Sophie's nap, Leah went out to the back steps to shell peas. The sun had swung around, off the stairs, but the heat rose, still and stifling and smelling of dirt from the earth in the backyard. Leah knew that the meal she had planned for this party was too elaborate, was taking too much of her time; but she knew, too, that she had organized it this way in part so that she could stay away from Anita and Greg and a vague feeling of anxiety they roused in her. She was glad to have this job to do, to be able to leave the house and come out here alone to sit.

Greg and Anita had had a small, quickly suppressed argument just before Sophie's nap, and Leah frowned, thinking of it, as her thumbnail slid along the seam of a bright-green peapod. She and Anita had been working in the kitchen, and Sophie was standing on a stool by the sink, playing quietly with the soapy water Anita had run for her. She was wearing only her Pampers, and she carefully poured water from one plastic container to another in the sink. Her fat protruding belly glistened with what she had spilled on it.

Greg came into the room and began to play with her. Leah stopped what she was doing for a moment to watch them. He was wearing only cut-off shorts, and his brown body, with the big bones moving under the skin, gave her as much pleasure as Sophie's translucent roundness did. She remembered how homely Greg had been just before he entered his teens, a fat child who wasn't popular and who stammered in any new situation. Once he had used her razor to shave his eyebrows off. He hated the way he looked, he had said when she asked him why. "And this is better?" she countered in a tense, shrill voice. He had looked at her as though he'd like to kill her in some slow and painful way.

"Y-y-y-y-yes," he said, his eyes not blinking under his smooth, naked forehead.

Greg made a waterfall, he blew bubbles with a straw he found in a kitchen drawer. Leah watched his muscular back, looked at Sophie's compact and delicate body on the stool next to him.

"Why can't you leave her alone for just a few minutes, Greg?" Anita said.

Leah looked away quickly; went back to peeling boiled potatoes for a salad.

"Why *should* I leave her alone?" Greg asked, standing straight. He shook the bubbly water from his fingers.

Anita's voice strained to be casual, reasonable. "Because you never do. She's perfectly content, playing by herself. And you always have to charm her with *your* game, your . . ." There was silence for a moment. "I just don't think it's good for her," Anita said finally.

Greg stood next to Sophie, looking at Anita. Leah looked at her too. She was staring over Sophie's head at Leah's son, with eyes that were free of love, free of any response to his beauty.

"Bupps, Daddy?" Sophie said. She had fished the soggy straw out of the water and held it up to Greg.

"Not now, honey," Greg said. He walked toward the door, his sense of injury apparent in the way he held his shoulders.

"Bupps!" Sophie shrieked after him. "Bupps," she wailed, and then bent over and cried, loudly and dramatically, with her head touching the counter, her face hidden against her small fat hands.

"Whoo," Anita said, moving toward her daughter and raising her eyebrows for Leah's benefit. "Naptime for this kidlet."

When Leah finished shelling the peas, she picked up the pot and the colander and went back into the kitchen. She glanced through the doorway into the living room. Greg lay on the floor, alone, reading an old issue of *Sports Illustrated*. Leah realized she hadn't seen Greg and Anita touch each other since they arrived.

Leah's house was like all the others around it, only with a slightly different "porch treatment" in front. It was part of a cheap suburban tract. She had bought it three years after she and Greg's father had been divorced, a year after she'd started teaching at the high school. The development was to have extended into the field and woods behind it, but by the time she and Greg had moved in, the first group of eight houses was already having trouble with its septic tanks. Until the town extended its sewer lines out as far as the development, which it didn't have any apparent intention of doing, no more houses could be built. Thus Leah had an unexpected park behind her. Deer sometimes wandered into her yard in the dusky mornings while she had her solitary breakfast; and on winter nights she occasionally went outside and listened to the snow fall with a hissing sound into the woods.

Anita's picnic was going to be at the bottom of the meadow, twenty or so feet before the woods started. They would be close enough to the house to hear Sophie if she cried, but far enough away so their noise wouldn't bother her.

While Greg got Sophie ready for bed and the steady pulse of the pump forcing water for Anita's shower thrummed through the house, Leah carried quilts and pillows, candles, and load after load of food and wine and beer down to the bottom of the lawn. She had changed into a dress and she had her shoes off and the grass felt cool and damp on her bare feet. Although it was still light outside, twilight had begun in the house, and she turned on the lamp in the kitchen as she assembled the final load from the clothes remaining in the hamper. Then she stayed outside, on her back on the faded and stained quilt, a glass of white wine within reach.

Greg called her and she answered halfheartedly, but she knew he couldn't hear her and she didn't get up. After a while the screen door smacked shut. She looked up and saw him walk across the grass to her. Over his cutoffs he wore a T-shirt that said "Computer programmers do it Digitally." He had worked for Digital since he'd graduated from Rutgers, since he'd married Anita.

"God, you did everything, Mom."

Leah propped herself up on an elbow. "I wanted to be able to just lie here without thinking about having to get up in a while to help."

"But you should have called me." He sat down on a pillow and reached into the cooler for a beer.

"Honey, you don't have to help with everything." And you shouldn't, she wanted to say. You shouldn't. She thought suddenly of all the years she had made him help her with the housework, even when she could have done it more efficiently herself; of all the times she'd lectured him on his responsibility to their tiny household. She had a vague, apologetic sense now that it had all been wrong, wrongheaded.

"What do you think," she asked, looking up at the first faint stars in the white sky, "was the thing that attracted you and Anita to each other in college?" She was embarrassed by the question as soon as she'd asked it, and rushed to qualify it. "I mean, looking back," she said.

He was saved from having to answer by the sound of a car in the driveway. "Ah. Guess who?" he said, and smiled. He got up and disappeared around the corner of the house, carrying his beer. She could hear voices raised in greeting, and in a minute they all appeared, Greg and Pete, and Pete's wife, Debby. Debby had been a student of Leah's years before. She was a sweet, stupid girl, with enormous breasts. She had had to marry Pete before she finished her junior year of high school. At the party Greg had thrown for them a few weeks after the wedding, Leah had found Debby crying in the bathroom; had cleaned up the vomit which had missed the toilet; and had tucked the miserable sixteen-year-old bride into her own bed for the night, while the noise of the party continued below.

They were cheerful now as they sat down and got beer and wine to drink. Pete told Leah how pretty she looked, and she made the mocking face she used at school when a student tried to flatter her. This teacherly manner had been her defense ever since Greg's friends began to turn into men suddenly, when she was alone and in her mid-thirties. It was like a joke they had all shared, especially she and Pete, the wildest of the friends, who had been sexually alert at an age when Greg still seemed to be sleepwalking through life.

When the screen door banged again, and Anita in a gauzy white dress stood poised a moment and then floated down through the fading summer light to them, Leah looked over at Pete and caught a look of sexual appraisal on his face.

"The birthday girl," Leah said quickly. Anita smiled at them all and sank down in the swirl of her skirts next to Greg.

"Hello, hello, hello," she said to each of them and leaned prettily, a frail reed, against Greg's shoulder. "What is there for me to drink, sweetheart?"

Greg poured some wine for her, let her lean. But he didn't look at her or respond to her. Even though Leah knew Anita was posturing slightly for the guests, she was moved by the younger woman's beauty, and irritated by Greg's stubborn unresponsiveness to it. She had the sudden conviction, as she reached over to light the picnic lanterns she had brought out earlier, that he would lose Anita and his marriage, and so, of course, Sophie. Her eyes momentarily filled with tears. She lighted the lamps and began to pass around the wicker picnic plates.

Leah drank too much during the meal. She poured herself glass after glass of white wine. The food she had spent all day preparing seemed tasteless to her. She ate a few small bites of the first course and didn't even cut herself a piece of Anita's birthday cake.

After they'd finished eating and were stretched out, drinking wine and beer, Pete lit a joint and passed it around. Leah remembered that she'd heard from someone else, some other high school friend of Greg's and Pete's, that he was dealing in a small way. She wrinkled her nose at the smell and leaned out of the circle. She had tried grass once or twice at Greg's insistence when he was in college, but it only made her sleepy and slightly nauseated. She thought it made Greg and his friends boring and she had told him so. He had shrugged and said, "It's just the same thing I feel about you and your friends when you've all been drinking."

Now their voices grew slowly more subdued and intimate. Debby was hunched over her glass of wine, talking at length to

Greg, who nodded and nodded. Anita and Pete, more relaxed, giggled. Leah was sorry she hadn't invited Joe. She felt old and solitary, an observer. She wanted to clean up and go to bed.

She stood and walked slowly to the house, carrying her wine. At the kitchen door she looked back. The scene was beautiful in the yellow lamplight; and at this distance their soft voices seemed like a part of nature, like the sound of leaves in the wind, or the liquid murmur of a stream.

Leah went upstairs and looked a long time at herself in the bright light of the bathroom. Her eye makeup had smeared slightly. Her lipstick was gone. She pushed her hair back. Her face looked tired, weakened by age. She set down her wineglass and slowly washed her face, rinsing it over and over in the cool running water.

She went down the darkened hallway to Sophie's room. She stood just outside the doorway because Greg had told her that Sophie was a light sleeper. She listened to the child's regular breathing as she had listened to her son a thousand times when he was small. The air was full of the perfumed smell of Sophie's Pampers.

The screen door smacked shut downstairs. Sophie stirred; the plastic Pampers rustled gently. Voices whispered, there was soft laughter in the kitchen. Dishes clinked. Were they picking up? Leah should go down and help. Someone turned on the faucet and the pipes sang gently behind the cheap walls. She reached into the bedroom and slowly closed Sophie's door.

Leah went downstairs, and as she crossed the living room, she heard Anita's voice, thick with wine, grass, from the kitchen. "No, it's *not* that," she said. "It's just this endless mommy-daddy-baby shit. The endless threesomeness of it all. We always have to be so fucking responsible. It's as though I don't exist as a woman anymore."

And Pete's voice, slurred and soft. "I can't imagine that with you. If I were with you. I mean, I've always thought of you as one of the sexiest ladies I know."

Leah cleared her throat and then coughed, loudly enough, she hoped, to warn them she was about to intrude upon them. But when she stepped into the dimly lit kitchen in her bare feet, Pete was gently lifting Anita's hair from her face in what was unmistakably the beginning of an embrace.

"I'm here," Leah said stupidly. Pete's hands leapt back as if burned. Anita turned slowly, foggily, toward Leah and smiled. The orange light glowed behind her and Leah could see she wasn't wearing a bra under the gauzy dress. Let her be drunk enough not to remember, Leah thought.

"Are you starting to clean up?" she asked brightly. "I'll go outside and get some more." She turned quickly away from them.

Outside it was cooler. She stood a moment by the back door. The air itself lifted her spirits slightly; but as she approached Greg, she felt the return of her sense of helpless sorrow for him.

He and Debby sat on the quilt, talking like two earnest children. They didn't notice Leah for a moment at the edge of the lantern light, and Debby went on talking, telling Greg how much trouble she'd had getting her youngest child to give up a pacifier.

Then Debby looked up and saw her. "Leah," she said. "It's Leah."

There was a pause as they both looked at her. In the still evening air Leah could hear crickets, the clatter of dishes in the kitchen.

"Mom. Oh. You looked so weird to me." Greg stared at her with amazed, stoned intensity, and Leah bent down to start loading the hamper. "For a minute I thought," he said slowly, "I mean, I really thought, when I looked at you, that I was about ten years old again."

Later, after Pete and Debby had left, Leah sat on the edge of her bed upstairs and listened to Greg and Anita below in the living room. She heard the low metallic shriek that meant they were pulling out the foldaway bed, the lazy alternation of their voices. Then Anita's took over, a pressured monologue, with an occasional sharply articulated word—"never," or "fucking"—that floated up through the night air and the thin walls of the house.

He didn't answer. Leah wanted him to. She sat in her room and listened to the sound of her son's marriage and wanted him to shout, to push, to hit. She thought of how he had sat, mute and resentful, when she had spoken just this way to him a hundred times, over the garbage not taken out, the bike not locked, the car dented, the curfew defied; thinking always that she was teaching him, teaching him the right way, the responsible way to get through life.

When she tiptoed past the living room on her way out, she heard them making love. The couch squeaked to their rhythm, he cried out in bewildered wild whispers, and there was a low mournful keening from Anita. They still had that, then. Did it make the rest easier? Harder? Leah remembered that she and Greg's father had made love, weeping, the night before he moved out of her life and Greg's forever.

For a moment, as she walked silently across the kitchen, she worried about leaving the house, about what seemed like an abandonment of Greg, of them all. But she had no power anymore—had never had the power, although at one time she thought she did—to stave off ruin, to guard her son against his share of pain. And for herself, right now, she wanted Joe. She wanted, just as Greg did, the illusion of wholeness, of repair, the broken parts fitting.

As she stepped outside and turned to shut the door, the porch light falling into the kitchen gleamed on the silver wrapping of the bread Joe had given her, the gift she'd forgotten to take to the party.

# Calling

At the very beginning he used to call her sometimes just to hear her voice. She'd say hello in that soft midwestern tone, and he'd listen—listen to hear whether she had a record on, or there were voices in the background, or there was just silence; and then he'd hang up. At first he told himself that he did it so he could imagine more clearly what she was doing when she wasn't with him. But he knew it didn't really help. If a record was playing, for instance, he'd find himself later wondering whether she'd been dancing with someone in her tiny apartment, as they had done on one of their first nights together. Or if there were voices, he'd wonder who it was, why she hadn't asked him over too. Was it a party, or had people just stopped by? Had she made dinner for them? He thought of the dinners she'd made for him, the various dishes she'd served him, and wondered if she'd cooked any of the same things.

After her apartment was robbed, he knew he ought to stop

calling. Whoever had broken in—well, they'd hardly *broken* in; she admitted she'd left the door unlocked by mistake when she went out—had taken only a few pieces of cheap jewelry. But he, or she, had ripped the apartment up a little, had poked through things *he* might have looked at if he'd been in her apartment alone—letters, diaries, photographs.

She was upset. She worried that the thief might come back, especially since he hadn't taken several valuable things which were sitting out in plain view—a portable TV, a silver vase. When he called right after the robbery, he could hear the tension in her voice on the phone. And once she said, "Look, whoever this is, will you please, please, please *stop* this. Stop calling, please." He could tell that she was near tears and he felt very bad for her as he hung up.

Sometimes, when he was with her, he'd ask, "Still getting those calls?" Once she asked him if he would answer the phone if it rang in the night. "Maybe if he hears a man's voice, he'll stop calling. Maybe it's one of those nuts who just picks a female name at random from the phone book because he thinks that means she's, you know, unprotected."

He had put his arm around her then, told her he'd always protect her. She was silent, as she often was when he seemed to be making some kind of claim on her.

Once she got a call when he was there. She picked up the phone and said hello. Then after a moment she set it gently back down in its cradle.

"Who was that?" he asked.

"Oh, it was another one of those freaky calls," she said. "You know, the usual breathing then hang up routine."

He asked her again why she didn't just come and stay at his place for a week or two, and she said, as she always did, that she wasn't going to let some pervert, some crazy, drive her out of her apartment.

When he thought about that call afterward, he was at first glad of it, because its happening to come when he was with her made it less likely that she'd ever suspect that the other calls came from him; but then he began to wonder who it was, who else she was seeing who might feel about her as he did. He suggested she talk to someone from the phone company about tracing the calls.

The phone company wasn't very helpful. They said there wasn't much she could do besides changing her number. But they asked her to keep a log of the calls for a few weeks—what time each one occurred, what she was doing at the time, and what the call consisted of. He looked at the log after the first two weeks. They were all his calls, he was pretty sure, all made at ten-thirty or eleven at night so he wouldn't wake her, disturb her sleep.

She had initials by some of the calls. He asked her what they meant. She said they were initials of friends who were over when she received the calls. He looked carefully at the initials. He couldn't figure out who all of them were, and that bothered him.

He asked her why she hadn't recorded the call she had gotten when he was there.

"Because that happened before I started the log, before I called the phone company."

He told her he thought it was important that she record all the calls she could remember, and so, reluctantly, she wrote down the day and approximate time of that call, and put his initials by it. That made him feel better.

By now she was seeing him only one or two nights a week. When he pushed for more time, she said that even if she was free she wouldn't see him more than that, that she didn't want to be seeing anyone that often. He accused her of having found someone else; she said that wasn't it, although it wasn't his business whether or not she *was* seeing someone else. She said she just needed privacy, time of her own. She said he was crowding her.

One night when she wouldn't see him, he went out to a bar alone, something he almost never did, and got drunk. He wasn't quite sure how he got home, but when he did, he called her. He knew it was much later than he usually called, but he wasn't sure how much later.

She didn't answer. He went into his bedroom and looked at the clock. It was one. Where was she? Who was she with? He called her again, and let it ring twenty or thirty times. He hung up.

He thought of how once when they were making love in the afternoon the phone had started to ring and she had moaned, "please, please," as though at the same time telling him to go on and the phone to stop. He called her again, but hung up after only one or two rings. She just wasn't home. It was obvious.

But then he was sure she *was* home, she was home with someone else on the mattress on the floor. When he made love with her, the mattress hitched slowly across the bedroom so that he'd wake up sometimes with the windows in an unfamiliar place and wonder, momentarily, where he was. He called her again and let it ring on and on.

He lost track of how many times he called her, but then, finally, he got a busy signal. The sharp sound startled him, made his heart beat strangely. He dialed again, and got the busy signal again.

He called the operator and said he thought the phone was broken, and it was an emergency, he needed to get through. She tried the number for him and said it wasn't broken, it was just either busy or off the hook. He called it again four or five more times before he fell asleep, but he always got the busy signal.

Late the next morning he stopped by her apartment. He had just gotten up and he knew he looked bad. His eyes were bloodshot and the lids were puffy. He felt tired and weak. She let him in and gave him coffee. She was wearing the old terry-cloth blue bathrobe that he liked. The coffee was so strong he could barely drink it.

"I got drunk last night," he told her. "Just flat-out too much booze. What'd you do?"

"I went to a concert with Frannie," she said.

"Good concert?" he asked.

"It was wonderful," she said. "They did the sixth Brandenburg Concerto, clearly the best one."

"Then what'd you do?"

"Not much. I went over to her house for a minute. Had some wine." She poured herself another cup of coffee and sat down at the table opposite him. She looked out of the apartment window at the dead geranium on her fire escape. A sparrow stood on the rim of the pot and puffed itself up.

"Then what?" he asked.

She looked at him a moment. "Came home. Went to bed." She shrugged. "And I got a bunch of those weird calls last night. Starting really late. I didn't answer 'cause the phone wasn't plugged in in my room—I had it out in the kitchen—and I didn't want to wake all the way up and go out in the kitchen just to have some asshole *breathe* on me."

"Oh, that's right," he said. "You have that kitchen thing." He looked over and saw that the phone was still plugged in in the kitchen.

"But this guy just kept *calling*. I'd sort of drift back to sleep, and then five minutes later it'd ring again. Sometimes just a few times, sometimes for a couple of minutes. So finally I came in here and just took the thing off the hook. I don't know." She shook her head. "I might have to change the number."

He offered to spend the night that night, but she said she had other things to do. She sounded irritated by the offer. They talked for a while more, and then she told him he had to go, she was going out.

The next day, she called him. She said she knew it would sound crazy, but she had what she called an "emotional conviction" that it had been him calling her the night before.

He laughed. His heart was pounding. "What makes you think so?" he asked.

"I don't know. Just the way you were talking yesterday, I guess," she said. "I don't really *think* so, though," she said. "I know so. It's true."

He was silent a moment.

"It *is* true, isn't it?" she said. "I just want you to tell me it's true."

"And do you think it was me the other times?" he asked.

"The other nights?" she said.

"Yes."

There was a long silence on the phone and he was sorry he'd asked.

"Well, you were with me for a couple of those calls," she said. "Weren't you?"

"Yeah, a couple," he said.

"Are you going to answer my question?" she asked.

"What question?"

"Were you the one calling the other night?"

"Well, I was pretty drunk," he said. "But I don't remember calling you."

"So it *might* have been you." Her voice was sarcastic.

"*Might* have. But I'm pretty sure it wasn't."

"Well, I'm pretty sure it was, and I want you to tell me, one way or the other, if it was you. That's what I want," she said.

"Look," he said. "I don't know what kind of need you have to think that it was me making those calls, but if you want to believe it, go ahead."

There was silence on the line. Then she said, "So it was you?"

"You know what I'm going to do in about a minute? I'm going to hang up on you. I don't have to listen to this stuff."

"Go ahead," she said. "Let me hear you hang up on me."

He was silent for a moment. "I don't want to hang up," he said. "This is ridiculous. Can't we stop it?"

"I'll stop when you tell me you made the calls."

"I'm not going to tell you that. Why would I have called you like that, again and again?"

"I don't know. Because you're jealous? Because you're crazy? Because you thought you'd catch me in bed with someone else? Why?"

"I don't know."

"But you called."

"No! No, I didn't call."

"Well, I'm sorry. I know it was you."

"But how do you know? What's your evidence?"

"I'm not talking about *evidence,*" she said. "I'm talking about what's true. I don't have to offer *evidence* to you. I know this. I know it's true. You. Made. The calls. That's all. Just say it. Just say, 'I made the calls.' That's all I want you to do."

"But I didn't. I wouldn't do something like that."

She didn't say anything for a moment. Then she said, "That's a nice *idea* to have about yourself. I feel that way about myself, too. But I want you to talk about what happened. I want you to say, 'I made the calls.' "

He thought for a moment. "What'll happen if I say I did?"

"You will have told the truth," she said.

"I'm sorry," he said. "I can't say that."

She hung up.

For a long time he sat with the phone in his hand, not thinking about anything. Then he realized that he was listening hard to the piercing beep coming over the line, that it was making him feel dizzy, sick to his stomach.

On and off through the day he thought of calling her again, of telling her what he thought of her. He could imagine calling and just saying "bitch" or "cunt," and hanging up. But thinking about it brought back that same sick feeling.

Two nights later, he had a few drinks and he called again. It was around ten-thirty. The phone rang twice, then a computerized voice came on the line and said that the number he was calling had been disconnected. He was startled by the unexpected sharp voice. It repeated its message. He hung up. He dialed the operator. She said yes, that number had been disconnected.

Was there a new number? he asked.

Yes, she said, but at the request of the customer, she wasn't allowed to release it.

He called her number three or four more times that night, and always the computerized voice came on, and always it told him twice over, firmly and clearly, what he already knew.

After that, he called once or sometimes twice nearly every night, even though he knew what to expect. It wasn't until three or four weeks later, until he'd met someone else, that he stopped.

# Expensive Gifts

Charlie Kelly was her eighth lover since the divorce. He was standing naked in silhouette, as slim as a stiletto in the light from the hall, rifling through the pockets in his jacket for his cigarettes. The sight of him gave Kate no pleasure. She hated the smell of cigarette smoke in her bedroom. She hated the horrible silence that fell between men and women who didn't know each other well after making love, but she hated even more for it to be filled with the rustling little rituals of the smoker.

"I'm afraid there are no ashtrays in here," she said. Her voice was pinched and proper. Five minutes before, she had been expelling short, pleased grunts, like a bear rooting around in garbage.

"That's okay," he said, sitting on the bed again, and lighting up. "My wineglass is empty."

"Actually," she said, although she wasn't at all sure of it, "that was *my* wineglass. And I was going to get some more wine." She stood up on her side of the bed and smashed her head on the Swedish ivy. She usually occupied Charlie's side of the bed. She wasn't used to the pitfalls on the other side. He appeared not to have noticed her accident.

"Here," she said, reaching over for the glass. "I'll bring you a real ashtray." He handed over the expensive wineglass, one of her wedding presents. The cardboard match leaned at an angle within it, its charred head resting in a tiny pool of red liquid. Kate felt Charlie's eyes upon her as she walked away from him, her slender silhouette now harshly revealed in the glare of the hall light. Her gait felt unfamiliar to her, awkward.

In the kitchen she threw the match away and set her glass down. She wanted to check Neddie. He always kicked the covers off in the intense private struggles that dominated his dreaming life, and he had a bad cold now. Kate dressed him for bed in a big sleeper that probably made a blanket unnecessary, but she still had a mystical belief in tucking him in, in pulling the covers right up to his chin.

The night light was on in his room, a tiny leering Mickey Mouse head that leaked excess light from a hole where its nose had been until Ned knocked it off with a toy one day. The covers had slid sideways off the bed into a tangled heap on the floor, and Neddie lay on his stomach. His hands were curled into fists, and one thumb rested near his open mouth, connected to it by a slender, almost invisible cord of saliva. His breathing was labored, thick with mucus.

Kate bent over him to tuck the covers in on the far side. Her breasts swung down and brushed his back. He muttered in his sleep, and reinserted his thumb in his mouth. He sucked briefly, his throat working too, in the same thorough way he'd pulled at her breast when he was still nursing; but he couldn't breathe. His mouth fell open after a moment, and his thumb slipped out. His face puckered slightly, but he slept on. Kate watched his face smooth out, and stroked his hair back.

She stopped in the kitchen and poured herself a new glass of wine. She looked briefly and halfheartedly for an ashtray for

Charlie, but settled, finally, on a saucer. She didn't want to return to her bedroom and make polite conversation with him. She wanted to call Al, her ex-husband, and talk comfortably; to make a joke of Charlie's stylized flattery of her and her own dogged unresponsiveness. But she couldn't have called him anyway. Al was getting married again soon. He'd fallen in love with his lab assistant, a dark, serious woman, and she would be sleeping there beside him.

She had called Al frequently in the two years since he'd moved out. Usually it was late at night, often she was drunk. Almost always it was after she'd been with someone else for an evening. Though they had fought bitterly in the year before they separated, the year after Neddie's birth, they were kind and loving in these drunken phone calls; they commiserated on the difficulties of a single life.

"Jesus," he'd said to her. "I can't seem to get the hang of anything. All the goddamn rules have changed. Either I'm a male chauvinist pig or I'm being attacked by an omnivorous Amazon, and I'm always *totally* surprised. No wonder those statistical people remarry so fast."

There was a silence while she thought of Al attacking, being attacked. He was small and slender, with curly brown hair and thick, wire-rimmed glasses which he removed carefully before starting to make love. They left two purplish dents like bruises on the sides of his nose.

"Oh, I don't know. It seems to me the main thing to remember is that there just aren't any rules anymore. You just have to do what makes you feel comfortable and good about yourself."

"Oh, Katie. You've been taking those *wise* pills again." She didn't respond. He cleared his throat. "Well, how about you? You feeling good about what you're doing?"

Kate had thought about the evening she had just spent. Her voice rose to a dangerously high pitch as she said "No" and started to cry.

Now she carried her wine and the saucer back to Charlie. Her bedroom had been a sun porch in some previous life. Two of its walls were a parade of large, drafty windows. As if to compensate, the landlord had installed huge radiators the entire length of one of these walls; they clanked and hissed all winter long, and made her room the warmest in the apartment. Kate had hung the lower halves of the windows with curtains that moved constantly in the free-flowing air currents. She liked to lie in bed and look out the naked top panes at the sky. It had been a luminous soft gray earlier, and now thick flakes, a darker gray against its gentle glow, brushed silently against the panes.

"Look," she said to Charlie, handing him the saucer. He was lying on his back with the open Marlboro box on his chest, using the lid for an ashtray.

"Yeah, I saw. It's sticking too, and I don't have snow tires. I'm going to have to leave pretty soon."

She looked away so he wouldn't see relief leap into her eyes. "It's so pretty, though. I almost feel like waking Neddie up to show him. He doesn't really remember it from last year. It's all new to him again. Can you imagine that?"

Charlie put out his cigarette in the saucer.

"You must be freezing your ass off." Kate was standing by the windows, watching the snow's straight descent. "Slide in here, lady, I'll warm you up."

She turned obediently and got in, but she said, "My father had a dog named Lady once. A collie. Horrible barker. He finally had someone shoot her. She just wouldn't shut up." None of that was true, but Kate didn't like to be called "lady."

Kate was, in fact, a reflexive liar. She hated to be unpleasant or contradictory, and when she felt that way, a lie, fully formed almost before she began to think about it, fell from her lips. Her husband had had a knack for recognizing them—he'd said it was as though her voice resonated slightly differently—and he would simply repeat them slowly so she could hear them herself, and tell him what was making her angry. Once in a fight about whether Al should work less and help her more with Ned, she had cried out, "Ned is wonderful because I've given up my fucking *life* to him!" His patient echo had made her weep, because her claim seemed at once the truth and a terrible lie.

Now Charlie tried to pull her over to him, but she said, "Ah, ah," and held up her full wineglass as an explanation. She took a sip. He turned away to get another cigarette.

"The kid all right?"

"What, Neddie?"

"Yeah, is that his name? Is he okay?" He leaned back with the cigarette in his mouth, and exhaled two long plumes of smoke from his nostrils. Kate thought about how the pillows would smell after he'd gone.

"He's sound asleep, but really stuffed up."

"How old is he?"

"He's just three."

"Cute age," said Charlie, tapping his cigarette on the saucer. "I've got two, you know."

"Two kids?" She was surprised. He nodded. "I would never have guessed that about you, Charlie. You're too much the gay blade, the town rake."

He grinned appreciatively. He worked at it, and liked to know his efforts were successful. "They're in Connecticut with my ex-wife."

"Do you see them often?"

"About once a month, I guess. She's remarried, so they've got a whole family scene there, really. It doesn't seem so important anymore. They're pretty much into their life, I'm pretty much into mine, you know."

"Yes," she said. They sat in what she imagined he thought was companionable silence. Two used parents. She had an old iron bedstead with a large ornate grille for a headboard and a smaller one at the foot. Charlie's head had slipped into the space between two of the white-painted rods. They pushed his ears forward slightly. He looked a little like the Mickey Mouse night light in Neddie's room. She smiled. She wondered why she had been so excited about going out with him tonight. When he'd finished his cigarette, he reached for her again. She set her wineglass down on the floor by her side of the bed and they made love. Charlie seemed interested in some variations on their earlier theme, but she shook her head no, no, and their lovemaking was short and somewhat neutral in character. Just as he pulled limply and stickily away from her to find another cigarette, Neddie's agonized shout floated back through the apartment to her. She leapt out of bed, upsetting her half-empty wineglass but avoiding the plant this time, and sprinted into the light and down the long hallway, pushing her breasts flat onto her chest to keep them from bouncing painfully.

Neddie's eyes were still shut. He had turned over onto his back and tears ran down his cheeks, into his ears. The covers were piled on the floor. "Nooo, monkey!" he moaned, and thrashed. Kate picked him up and cradled him close, his wet face pressing on her neck.

"Neddie, it's Mommy. Mommy's here now. *No* monkeys. The monkeys are all gone. You're in your room, Neddie, with Mommy, see?" She pulled her head back to look at him. His eyes were open now, but he looked blank. She walked around the room with him, talking slowly.

"We're at home, Neddie. You had a dream. That wasn't real. That silly monkey was a dream. See, here's Sleazy. He's real." She pointed to Ned's bear, sitting on a shelf. Ned reached for him. "Sleazy," he said, and tucked him in close under his chin, just as Kate held him. She shifted him to her hip now, and went around the room, showing him all his favorite things. Kate was tall and thin. She had down-drooping breasts and flat, narrow hips. She looked like a carved white column in the dim light.

"And look, Ned. Look what's happening out here." She carried him to the window. The flakes danced thickly in a sudden gust of wind under the street light outside Ned's room, a thousand suicidal moths. "Do you know what that is?"

"Dat's da snow!" he said. His mouth hung open and his breath was hot and damp on her breast.

"And it's all piling up on the ground, Neddie, see? And tomorrow we can find the sled that Daddy gave you in the basement, and put on boots and mittens . . ."

"And my hat?" Ned wore a baseball hat every day. He watched her face now to be sure they were in agreement on this.

"Yeah, your hat, but you have to pull your hood up over it to keep your ears warm. And we can play all day because tomorrow's Sunday. Mommy doesn't have to work."

"Not day care?"

"No, tomorrow we can stay home *all* day. Okay?" They watched the snow together for a moment. Then she turned from the window. "I'm going to tuck you in now." She carried the child to his bed and started to lower him. His legs and arms gripped her tightly, a monkey's grip.

"Stay here, Mumma."

"Okay." He relaxed, and let her put him down on the bed. "But Mommy's cold. You move over and make room for me under these covers." He wiggled back against the wall and she slid in next to him and pulled the covers over them both. His face was inches from hers. He smiled at her and reached up to pat her face. His hands were sticky and warm. "Mumma," he said.

"Yes," she said, tenderly, and shut her eyes to set a good example for him. Sometime later she woke to hear the front door shut gently, and footsteps going down the stairs. Then dimly, as at a great distance, or as if it were all happening in some muffled, underwater world, a car started up in the street, there was a brief series of whirring sounds as it struggled back and forth out of its parking place, and then, like a thin cry, its noise evaporated into the night.

When Neddie woke her, the sky was still gray. The light in the room was gray too, gentle and chaste. The snow had stuck in the mesh of the summer screens left on the windows, and the house seemed wrapped in gauze. It still fell outside, heavy and soft, but from somewhere on the street came the *chink, chink* of a lone optimist already shoveling.

"Ned. Let me sleep a minute more."

"You already sleeped a long time, Mumma. And I *need* you."

He was standing by the bed, his face just above her head. He wore a red baseball cap, and his brown eyes regarded her gravely.

"Why do you need me?"

"You hafta make my train go."

"What, Granpoppy's train?" He nodded his head solemnly. "Oh, Christ!" she swore, and violently threw the covers back, swinging her legs out in the same motion. He looked frightened, and she felt instantly remorseful. "No, Neddie, it's all right. I'm just mad at the *train*. I'll fix it."

Her parents had given Ned the train, an expensive Swedish model of painted wood. The cars fastened together with magnets. Occasionally, by chance, Ned would line them up correctly, but most often, one or two cars would be turned backward, north pole to north pole, or south to south, and the more he would try to push them together, the more they repelled each other. Her parents' extravagance since her divorce, their attempts to ease her way and Ned's with things she didn't want, couldn't use, annoyed her. She must have bent down to correct the magnetic attraction on this thing thirty times since they'd given it to Ned.

He came and squatted by her. He had laid the track out and there were miniature pigs and sheep and ducks heaped up in the tiny open train cars. The thought of his working silently for so long, trying not to wake her, touched her. As they squatted together she began to try to explain to him the idea of polar attraction, turning the brightly painted cars first one way and then the other, so he could see the greedy pull at work.

Suddenly his head dipped slightly to look underneath her and his expression changed. She stopped. "Mumma's leaking?" he asked, pointing to the floor. She shifted her weight to one leg and looked on the floor under where she'd been squatting. Thick drops of whitish liquid, reminders of lovemaking the night before, glistened like pearls on the nicked wood. She laughed and stood up to get some Kleenex.

"It's all right, Neddie. Mommy can clean it up in a second. See?" she said. "All gone."

She smiled down at him as he squatted, fuzzy and compact in his sleeper, like a baby bear. He turned away and began to pull the toy train, now perfectly attached, around the expensive track.

# The Birds and the Bees

My mother had been a debutante. She had renounced her frivolous nature when she met my father, who was a scholar, and had once demonstrated to her the purity of his soul by pronouncing "boogie-woogie" with soft g's. They rushed to get married before the war because they assumed he would be sent abroad. But he had a bad kidney, it turned out. They settled down in New Haven while he finished his dissertation, and then moved to Chicago, where he got a teaching job, and she had me.

Sometimes after my father had gone to his office, she would play records of the songs she had danced to in her late teens. Even now when I hear Cole Porter tunes I can remember the rich sour scent of the cotton blanket I held against my cheek while I rested on the couch and watched my tall blond mother foxtrot slowly by herself around our living room.

My mother never got used to Chicago. Everything about it bothered her: the dirt, the congestion, the flat accents, and the danger. The danger both frightened and excited her. In the mornings my parents would sit in the yellow breakfast nook she'd created in a corner of the kitchen, and read the paper. My mother would say, "Did you see this? This man with the razor? It could have been *anyone,* just anyone passing by him!" Or: "Did you read about those three teenage girls? He might have walked right under our window on his way home!" She would shake her head, her eyes fierce, while my father grunted and read on in his section of the paper.

After I learned to read, she clipped that kind of story out of the paper so I wouldn't be exposed to such horrors. She saved the clippings for my father. Once a week or so he would read through them quickly and throw them away.

Once, playing outside on a wintry afternoon, I saw a bunch of them in our trash can and pulled them out. I smoothed them on the back steps with my wet mittens and read them as well as I could. They told of death by fire, hunger, jealous love. They told of other nightmares, which remained mysterious because of words I couldn't understand.

I had trouble fitting the world that opened to me with the image of my father at his desk impassively picking up one article after another and crumpling each as he finished, dropping it into the wastebasket like the discarded curved peel of an orange; or of my mother, humming to herself while she clipped them out with her sewing scissors, as busy and happy as when she cut through pattern tissue and wool to make me a new jumper.

Late one afternoon in the fall of the year I turned eleven, I got sick in school. When the abdominal cramps were so bad that I had to hold my breath, I raised my hand and asked to go to the bathroom. I worried that I might not make it down the three flights of stairs to the echoing basement where we lined up to pee before recess. Now it was deserted. My footsteps rang loudly. Even though I sat so long on the toilet that the black lines around the hexagonal tiles on the floor seemed to rise up several inches and form a wire screen, nothing happened. I wiped myself and nearly cried out when I saw the red stain on the paper. I went straight to the office and said I had to go home; I was sick. The principal at first resisted but finally acceded to the force of my terror. He called my home, and Mother said she'd be there waiting for me.

I was about halfway home, walking down the windy deserted street, when I felt liquid running down my leg. Bending over, I saw the dark blood make a jagged line on my calf. By the time I got home, the white socks my mother bought for me were stained brownish pink over my ankle bone.

At the door, I burst into tears and wordlessly pointed to my feet.

My mother, whose face had been anxious as I walked up the stairs to our apartment, smiled suddenly. "But, darling, it's your period! Your menstrual period," she said. She laughed, at me I felt, and I grew sullen.

"What's that?"

"*You* know, Ginny. It's the beginning of your being a woman."

"I *don't* know," I said furiously, blowing my nose.

Now my mother looked irritated. "Didn't you read that booklet I gave you?"

"What booklet?"

"Oh, I forget the title," she said crossly. "A little pamphlet thing. I think it was 'You're a Young Lady Now,' something like that. Don't you remember? I left it on your bedside table."

"Yes," I said. It had been illustrated with the same kind of drawings of contemporary scenes that were in my Sunday school pamphlets.

"Didn't you read it?"

"No."

"Well," she said. A vertical line appeared between her thick brows. "Well, I went to a lot of trouble to find that book. I wish when I gave you something like that you'd at least . . ." She trailed off and sighed. "You'd better get your coat off and we'll clean you up."

In the bathroom she knelt before me and helped me off with socks, shoes, underpants. I was mortified. I wished I had read the book. I would have done anything to avoid this scene. My mother's hair fell forward, and I looked down at the exposed back of her neck as she ran the washcloth briskly up and down my chafed legs, and worst of all, gently washed me *down there*. Then she outfitted me and carefully explained belts, pads, clots, cramps, all the while avoiding my eyes.

After I'd waked from a nap, she came and sat on the edge of my bed. Her hands, with their long nails painted the palest of pinks, moved over my bedspread as she talked, pulling at the little cotton tufts which made a design on it.

"Now that you're starting to be a woman, Virginia, I want to tell you something, and I want you to pay careful attention."

I licked my sleep-dried lips and nodded. I wished my father would come home and end the horrible intimacy into which this change in my body seemed to have betrayed me.

"I just want to tell you how careful you have to be now. I mean, I know you've always been a good girl, and done just what I told you, but it's even more important now, do you understand?" I nodded, in spite of my confusion. "Now, I know it must seem to you that you're still just a little girl, but you're not anymore, really. And even if someone should seem very nice, you mustn't pay any attention. Some man, I mean. You must remember that you are really a young woman. You just can't be too careful." Her voice thrilled a little in the same way it did when she talked about the newspaper stories. "Do you understand me?"

I didn't know what my mother was saying. It seemed a mystery that I would have to solve later. For now, I simply wanted her off my bed, out of my room. I nodded, and said yes, I understood. When she had gone, I lay silently until long after I heard my father come home.

It was a few months after this that Anna Solmitz moved into our building and became my first real friend.

Anna was tall and blond, like my mother, and big, almost fat, really. Her father taught at the university too. Her family had left Germany and lived in England during the war, and although her parents had German accents, Anna spoke with a British lilt I admired. She had lived in New York for several years, but they were planning to stay in Chicago now, she told me. We walked to and from school together each day and talked incessantly. We were a peculiar pair—she big and loud, and I small, dark and secretive. The other fifth graders were contemptuous of us: of me because my mother dressed me in such fancy clothes and I was the teacher's pet, and of Anna because she was fat and strange.

Anna hadn't had her first period yet and she didn't for several more years, even though she was almost exactly my age and so much bigger. She told me it was the custom in her family, when someone menstruated for the first time, to slap her hard across the face. She couldn't wait until it happened to her. When I thought about it later, I realized my mother had saved her confusing warning for me in just the way that Anna's mother was saving a slap for her.

Anna had a little brother named Freddie, who was two, and sometimes we baby-sat for him while her mother did a quick errand. I pretended to like Freddie, because Anna adored him. But secretly I was jealous of her affection for him and repulsed by him. His constant drooling, his piercing screams when he was angry or hurt, the horrible smell he carried around when his pants were full—he was utterly disgusting to me, and it seemed peculiar that Anna didn't share my feelings.

Once when I was alone in the Solmitzes' living room with him, I reached out and pinched his fat creased arm, twisting the bit of soft skin I held between my fingers. He looked at me stupidly for a moment, and then began to scream in short frantic bursts. Anna came running from the bathroom and picked him up. She asked me what had happened, and I said he fell. Within a few days, he seemed to have forgotten it and again played trustingly near me.

Anna and her parents all played instruments. Sometimes they would have little musical evenings, and invite a small number of friends. I hated to go to these. The punch and the cookies weren't sweet enough, tasted irrevocably foreign. And Anna, straddling her cello, absorbed in her music, a tiny mustache of perspiration glittering on her upper lip, embarrassed me. I knew my discomfort was misplaced, because my mother, whose nose wrinkled at the merest whiff of the indecorous, only admired Anna and her family for their artistry on these evenings. Nonetheless, I couldn't bear watching her with her legs spread wide, not even caring that people might be thinking of what they would see if the cello weren't there.

But I loved her so that I could forgive her anything. We slept over at each other's houses. We held each other tenderly in the dark and talked about our plans for a glorious life. Together also we pondered over another book my mother had given me, this time in consultation with Anna's mother. It talked about bees and pollination and, putatively, about how babies are made. It told us that the man had the seed and the woman the egg, but it never quite explained how they got together. Anna was sure that it happened in bed at night. She thought that when the man rolled over the woman, his seed dropped down onto her. We had seen a film in science class in which a male fish swam over the eggs a female had laid, and in rhythmic, convulsive spurts, shot out the seeds which floated slowly down to the iridescent eggs. It happened like that, she thought.

Then one day, on the way to school, as if to answer our questions, a graffito appeared on the walls of the viaduct under the IC tracks. It was huge. It must have taken the artist half the night. Drawn in loving detail, a nude man and woman stood next to each other. The man had an erection which loomed nearly as large as a third person between them. The woman was pointing to her ornate labia. A cartoon bubble appeared over her head. She said, "Stick it right in, honey."

As I remember, we didn't comment on this immediately, except to giggle because it was dirty. But on the way home, passing it again, Anna asked, "Do you think that's how they do it?"

"Make babies, you mean?"

"Yes, do you think? That the man puts his thing inside?"

We looked around to be sure that no one could hear us. I tried to think of my father and mother doing that. It was grotesque, impossible.

"No," I said.

We walked in silence down the gritty street. Ahead of us, a bigger boy was kicking a can as he walked along. She turned to me. "I think they do," she said. Tears glittered in her eyes.

We were shaken. It seemed cruel that this least probable of all possibilities we had discussed should be it. Hadn't we in fact dismissed it as too unthinkable, too unlike our parents? Particularly our mothers, both of whom knew so well what was ladylike and what was not. We made a pact to stay up and listen to them.

The two or three times I managed to stay awake until after my parents had gone to bed, there was a silence behind their door, broken only by a cough or, itself horrible enough, a fart. But Anna had more success. Sitting in the darkened hallway after everyone had gone to bed, she listened as first her parents talked for a while. Then she said she could hear them rummaging around in bed for a long time, the springs squeaking and bouncing; and then they made noises as though they were doing just what the picture under the IC said, just the noises you'd expect. Her mother cried out over and over, and finally her father grunted, like a big pig, several times. Anna crept back to her room and, huddling under her covers, she cried and cried.

Although I couldn't look Mr. and Mrs. Solmitz in the face anymore, I was glad it was they who had done it and not my parents. We had to accept this then as the answer to our mystery. But it presented a still deeper one: Why would anyone want to do such a thing?

We played mostly at Anna's house, because her mother was preoccupied with Freddie and left us alone. In her bedroom with the door shut, we began to act out the way we imagined it must be. Usually, Anna would be the man. She would grab me, and wrestle me down, sometimes even pulling my hair back. When she had pinned me, she would yank my skirt up and push her pubic bone against mine. It hurt. I would make the noises she had told me about. Sometimes she stopped me to correct the noise. "No, no," she would say, sounding like an English nanny. "Not so fast as that." Then she would grunt once or twice and we would roll away from each other, laughing hysterically. We often swore never to marry. We would live together, chastely.

When summer came, Anna and I began to break the rules. Her boundary lines were wider than mine, but we wandered even beyond them. Together we rode the IC downtown and walked along Michigan Avenue, eating ice cream cones among the adult shoppers and museumgoers. In defiance of polio and our mothers, we played in the crowds at the beach on Fifty-seventh Street. We crossed the Midway and wandered the fringes of the black ghetto. One day we went tree-climbing by the lagoon behind the Museum of Science and Industry. Afterward we lay together on the grass, slapping at the mosquitoes that bred there. Anna was wearing shorts, and her fat white legs were splotched with raised bites. She scratched at them until they bled.

As we walked along the bridle path on the way home, a man who had been walking behind us caught up. He was probably still a teenager, but he was a grownup to us, although he wore blue jeans, which the grownups in our world did not. He was small, not too much taller than Anna, and dark, with a shadowy stubble on his chin. Because he was good-looking, we were excited and pleased that he spoke to us. It was thrilling, too, to break the rule about talking to strangers.

He asked us to watch the path for him for a moment. He stepped into the bushes and although he had his back to us, we could hear urine splashing on the dead leaves and plants. We caught each other's eye and suppressed our giggles. He turned and came back toward us, his hands awkwardly crossed low in front of him. He had a gentle, high-pitched voice, and he talked to us, asking us where we lived, what we'd been doing by the lagoon, whether we'd been to the museum, what our favorite things there were. After a time, only I answered. I looked at Anna. She was staring at his front. His hands had dropped and he had an erection. It seems impossible that I hadn't noticed it, but I hadn't. Perhaps because it was so unlike what the picture under the IC had led me to expect. We stood in silence.

"Oh, this," he said. "Does it embarrass you?"

We were polite girls. In unison we shook our heads, the blond and the dark. I said, "No."

"Good. It's just that when it's big, up like this, it's more comfortable not to have it in my pants." I looked at it. It seemed very pink and rubbery, like some toy Freddie would have for his bath.

"You can touch it."

I heard Anna's sharp intake of breath. Neither of us moved. He stepped toward us. Anna stepped back. He reached out and took my hand, and put it on him. His skin was soft and dry, like silk. He moved my hand gently up and down. His hand was damp and warm, holding mine.

"You too," he said to Anna, but he was watching my face. I saw her hand come forward. Her fingers brushed him close to mine, and then her hand flew away. He let go of me and squatted by us. He asked us if we liked to play games. What games did we like to play? His face was lower than ours. I looked down at his penis. It seemed to point at me. Any game we liked, he said. Hide-and-seek?

Anna grabbed my hand. "We can't," she said, sounding very British. "We must go now. We must." She was pulling me back, away from him. He didn't get up or try to follow us. His eyes didn't leave mine. She jerked my arm and pulled me through the bushes out onto the street. We had been, all along, only thirty or so feet from Stony Island Avenue. A clump of people stood waiting for a bus on the corner, and a woman strolled past us with a baby carriage. I blinked in the bright light.

"Come *on* now," Anna squeaked. Her face was wet with tears. "We have to get away from here. Come on." She started to run, pulling me. I had trouble keeping up with her long strides. Once or twice she nearly pulled me forward over my own feet. She made a funny blubbering noise as she ran. We went to her apartment, straight into the bathroom, and locked the door.

"We have to wash our hands," she said. "Or we'll get infected, do you see?" She lathered her hands and passed the soap to me.

She seemed hardly aware of me. She was whispering to herself. Her face was streaked and blotched and clear liquid flowed like tears from her nose. She scrubbed furiously. "This won't do," she whispered. She grabbed the can of bathroom cleanser and sprinkled the powder on her hands. It formed a thick white paste with the soap as she rubbed it in. There was a small stiff brush on the sink, used for cleaning fingernails. Anna picked this up and fiercely scrubbed her hands. I watched until I could see the blood seeping up pink through the cleanser.

"That's enough, Anna," I said. "That's clean enough."

"We're in*fec*ted, oooh, we're infected," she whispered. A bubble formed and popped over her mouth. I took her hands and rinsed them under the spigot. I washed her face with a cool washcloth. We went into her room, and I lay with her on her bed until she was calm, although her eyes were red and her lashes still gummed with tears. We held each other and promised never, never to tell that we crossed Stony Island Avenue.

But Anna told. A week or so later, her mother warned her about the park. A little girl had been molested behind some bushes a few blocks from the museum. Anna asked what molested meant. Her mother explained it to her in a general way. Anna went into her room and thought for half an hour. Then she came out and told her mother she thought we had been molested too.

My mother was upset and furious and, for once, wanted to discuss with me exact details. "It comes from living in this horrible, horrible city," she said. "I wish I'd never heard of Chicago." She told me she was bitterly disappointed in me. She was shocked that I would disobey her, and hurt that I hadn't told her right away what had happened. "I always thought we had such a good relationship, Virginia; that we could talk about anything." I was sent to my room while the grownups decided what they would do. When my father got home, he came in and sat on my bed for a while looking sorrowfully at me, but I lay staring at the wall and kept my own counsel.

Anna and I were forbidden to go outside or to play together again that summer, and in August my mother took me to Connecticut for a month. But I saw Anna twice before that. Once the police came to talk to us, and showed us hundreds of pictures of men's faces. They all had numbered tags around their necks. And one other time we went to police headquarters downtown with our mothers to see if they'd found the right man. Both women were tight-lipped, and my mother was slightly tearful. Our part of the room was very dark. Anna and I looked at each other across our mothers' angry profiles. Her eyes seemed accusatory, and I looked away first.

The men came out onto a stage and stood with their toes on a marker. Bright lights shone on them, and they all looked startled and unclean. A policeman giving them instructions said something that made them all laugh, and the line they were forming disintegrated for a moment and then took shape again. When I saw that none of the men was the one who had molested us, my heart, which had felt as though a hand were gripping it tight, relaxed and expanded in my chest, and I was able to cry.

In the fall, Anna and I resumed our friendship. She didn't want to talk about the events of the summer, though. She had had many nightmares, and she was trying to forget them all. I thought of them often. What I remembered most clearly was the man's light voice, suffused with desperate tenderness, asking me to play, wouldn't I play? Whatever game I liked. Tiny beads of sweat had sat on his upper lip even though it wasn't a hot day; beads of sweat I could have reached down and touched as he squatted in front of me. I had thought I might reach out and run my finger gently across his upper lip, until Anna pulled my hand away and rescued me.

# The Quality of Life

Alan watched Jody bending to get something out of the refrigerator. As she straightened up, their eyes met and she smiled at him. "So it'll be one big happy family, huh?"

Alan nodded. He'd been married to Jody until two years earlier, and he still felt an odd sense of comfort as he sat in the kitchen of the house they'd shared, the house she still lived in. She had poured them both some wine while the children—the young people—finished getting their stuff together. He was taking them for the Christmas holidays.

"All her kids too?"

"What do you mean, *all,* Jode? She's only got three. Same as us."

She grinned. "It never seemed like *only* to me. Course in those days men weren't into all this *sharing,* all this communicating with their offspring. Weeks could go by . . ."

"Let's not," he said.

She looked at him quizzically. "What is it with you? You used to be good for a few laughs anyway."

He shrugged.

She sipped at her wine, then bent over the sink. Her hair, that even chestnut brown, fell forward and hid the side of her face. He wondered if she was touching it up now.

"What're you going to do?" he asked.

She swept her hair back with one hand and stared at him. "What do you mean?"

"For Christmas. For the holidays. Anything special?"

She smiled. "I'll think of something." She turned and started fussing with whatever there was in the sink. She was wearing a short-sleeved shirt, and he watched her bare arms move quickly, gracefully, the skin at her elbows creasing and puckering with her motion. Claudia's arms weren't like that. Not yet. He felt a sudden pang for Jody.

"Mom!" It was Andrea, their youngest, calling from the second floor.

Jody put her hands on her hips and arched her back slightly, a familiar, exaggerated posture of irritation. He watched the cords in her neck tighten as she yelled back, with slow and precise diction, "If you want to talk to me, please come to where I am so I *do not* have to shout to be heard."

"Oh, shit!" came the reply; but after a moment Andrea thundered down the stairs. Her hair flew in all directions. She ignored her father. She'd greeted him when he arrived, and besides, she wasn't able to sustain a conversation with both parents at once. Her voice boomed. "For Christ's sake, Mom. All I have is one little question and I've gotta come all the way down *here?*"

Alan stared at them. Even though the girl was bigger than her mother, she was narrow and snaky through the hips. Slender Jody, her eyes steady on her daughter, still conveyed the mysterious massiveness of a grown woman.

"I mean, doesn't that strike you as unreasonable?"

Jody didn't answer.

"Doesn't it?" Andrea persisted. She looked nervously at her father.

"What's your question?" Jody asked.

"Aaah!" Andrea shook her wild hair and stamped her foot in protest. Then asked her question. "Where are my painter's pants?"

"Check the dryer," Jody answered, and Andrea flung herself at the basement door and down the stairs.

"How'd her hair get like that?" he asked.

"Like what?"

"God, it's so . . . bushy. So fanned out."

"Oh. She braids it wet. Tiny little braids all over." They could hear Andrea in the basement, banging the dryer shut. She started up the stairs. "Our own sweet pickaninny," Jody said loudly. Andrea emerged with the painter's pants. "And when she wakes up and brushes it out . . . magic!"

Andrea scowled at her mother as she crossed the kitchen. She stopped at the doorway to the back hall. "And you know what else I wish, Mom?"

Jody looked at her. "No. What?" she asked calmly.

"I wish you would not talk about me in the third person as though I wasn't even *there*. It's just fucking *rude*, that's what it is." She left the hall, and they could hear her, heavy-footed on the stairs.

Jody sighed. "Sometimes I wish we had some sort of neutral drop-off point. An Ellis Island. A no-man's-land or something. Where we could work these exchanges better."

"Is that what's eating her?"

"I *think*. At any rate, she's usually actually kind of lovely. Foul-mouthed always. But really, the light of my life."

He looked up at her. She seemed to mean it. Behind the fall of her hair, she was chewing her lower lip. "She's the only one who touches me anymore," Jody said abruptly.

His younger son, Steven, a senior in high school, walked in. "Let's get this show on the road," he said. "It drives me nuts how long it takes to get anything to happen in this house."

"What's your rush?"

"Well, I don't know. I thought we were trying to go or something. Wasn't that the idea?" He looked at his father, who sat sprawled at the kitchen table, his legs stretched out in front of him. Alan had taken off his boots by the front door, and he wore wool socks of two different colors.

Jody went back to her work at the sink. Washing lettuce, that's what she was doing. She shook a handful of the wet green leaves and started to spread them on a cloth on the countertop.

Alan picked up his glass. "David's not ready anyway, is he? I haven't seen him."

"He's in the car," Jody said.

"What?"

"He's in the car. He was all packed when you came, and he took his bag out right away and he's sitting in the car. Come look."

He went over to the sink and stood next to her. His older son had the interior light on in the car, probably to read by. At any rate, his head was bent down and he sat motionless in the little yellow world. Jody was watching Alan's face, he could tell, and when he looked at her, she shrugged and grinned, as though embarrassed.

"Yeah. So all we need is Andrea," Steve said. He went out into the hall and up the stairs, calling for her.

"Why is he like that?" Alan said, gesturing out the window with his wineglass.

"There's nothing wrong with being like that," she said. "I used to be like that when I was a kid too." She was bent over the sink again, rinsing the lettuce. It was escarole, and the frilled green edges made it look as though she were working with some delicate fabric. "I just couldn't stand the amount of fussing it took to get us all aimed in one direction, so I'd just go sit by the front door till everyone was ready." Jody was one of four sisters, daughters of an Episcopal priest. Alan had actually dated another one of them, Christine, before he'd met Jody. She was stately, beautiful. But it had been tomboyish Jody, who then still chain-smoked

Camels and had a reputation for being wild, whom Alan felt relaxed with and finally chose. Christine had married a clergyman and moved to Minnesota.

Jody set more lettuce on the cloth, and tore off several paper towels to pat it dry with. "It's like on an airplane," she said. "You can rush and get all your stuff together and fuss around, and then stand in the aisles for ten minutes. Or you can just sit and read in comfort until the door is open and the aisle is clear."

"You're so smart," he said.

She grinned again. "Me and David," she said. "It's amazing, the persistence of family characteristics."

"Since you're so smart," he said, "why don't you get one of those twirling baskets that dries the lettuce off in a second, instead of using up all these paper towels?"

She looked at him a long moment. "I don't know what I'm supposed to hear," she said. "Is this the story of your concern about my finances? Or is this the story of how in later life you've become domestic, of how someone else has managed to do what I couldn't?"

"Oh, Jody," he said wearily. "You're not supposed to hear anything."

After a minute she said, "I'm sorry. It's just that there was a time when you wouldn't have noticed *what* I was doing with the goddamned lettuce. It's just so odd to me that now you do."

They could hear Steve and Andrea on the stairs.

"It's easier to notice everything now," he said. "Now that I don't live here anymore."

Steve was in the doorway. "We're ready. I think we're ready. I think we're really really ready."

"Let me come out and say goodbye," Jody said.

He felt an odd sinking, a sense of apprehension at leaving. He'd felt it before. Somehow, when he had the children, he didn't see them as clearly as he did when he was with Jody. It seemed that she knew them in a way he couldn't by himself, hadn't been able to since the divorce. Or maybe it was the house, their own house, and something about the way they felt free to move around in it, to yell up and down the stairs, to walk around carrying plates of food; which they didn't in the house he lived in with Claudia and her children, the expensive, carpeted house that was hers from her first marriage. When he was married to Jody, he was made miserable by the confusion, the lack of grace in his family life. But that disarray seemed elemental to his kids, and Alan had found nothing to offer them as a substitute.

He followed Jody into the hall, pulling his coat on. Andrea was cool to her, let Jody kiss her cheek. But Steve made noise the whole time—thank God for Steve!—and so it felt like a cheerful goodbye.

After Alan tied his boots, he turned to Jody. Steve and Andrea were outside. They could hear Steve singing a Christmas carol. "And David?" he asked. "Did you say goodbye to him?"

She nodded. "He did everything absolutely correctly. A kiss, a Christmas present, the works."

"Well, then, Merry Christmas," he said.

"To you too," she said. "I hope it's great fun."

"Thanks," he called back, already walking to the car.

He got in and started the engine. Andrea and Steve had gotten in the back seat, their bags between them. As he turned out of the driveway, Andrea rolled down her window and called, "Bye, Mom! Bye, Mommy!"

He looked back. Jody was silhouetted in the doorway, and her hand came up to wave.

There was silence in the dark car. He said, "I feel a little bad for Mom, taking all you kids away from her for the holiday."

"I wouldn't," Steve said. "She'll have a great time."

"What do you mean?"

Andrea piped up, "She gets to go to the Carib*be*an with that guy, and we all have to stay around *here!*"

"It's Ca*ri*bbean," David said in his flat voice, without turning.

"Who cares?" Andrea said. "I don't care."

"I think you can pronounce it either way, Dave," Steve said.

David shrugged. "*Eye*ther way," he said.

"Wait a minute. She's going away?" He felt a sense of indignation rising.

"She's going to the Caribbean with this guy she's been *dating,*" Andrea said. She pulled herself forward behind him and he could feel her damp breath on his neck. "She's going to be all warm and come back tanned and—"

"But she didn't tell me," he said. "I mean, what if something happened? If we needed to get in touch with her?"

"We've got her address, Dad," David said. "In fact, she gave each of us the name of the hotel and the telephone number, in case one of us lost it."

Alan looked over at David, who stared levelly back.

"She's going with a guy named Floyce Hutchinson," David said. "He's a developer. Big bucks." David was watching him, he could tell.

His voice was casual. "Nice guy?" he asked.

"Who cares?" Andrea said. "She's going to be warm, and we have to stay here in this shitty winter and *freeze* for ten days."

In his mind's eye, Jody washed the pale-green escarole, sometimes pausing to hook her falling hair back over one ear. He should have thought. You didn't make fancy salads just for yourself. *Jody* didn't anyway. Sometimes during their marriage he had accused her of having forgotten how to cook altogether. Often, if she was engrossed in a book, she'd just open a few cans of soup for dinner and tell the children they could read at the table too. Alan had hated that, those silent meals with bread and sandwich fixings not so much arranged as *tossed* on the table; and the intermittent sibilant flip of someone's page the only human noise besides chewing, swallowing.

He had wanted the divorce. Jody had argued against it, but most of her arguments had to do with the children. He had pointed this out to her, told her it was part of the problem as far as he was concerned. She had conceded, finally, that she didn't have much energy for him. "But it's not all meant to be fun," she had said. "There's got to be some pain too, if it's real. I saw this as part of the long haul." Tears were running down her face.

Several times he'd had to get her to lower her voice so she wouldn't wake the children, who were sleeping upstairs. "For this bunch of years it's the kids, the jobs. *Later* I thought maybe we'd be sexy again."

Later was too late, he told her. And then he told her about Claudia.

She was angry. She threw a salt shaker at him. She called him an idiot, an asshole. She predicted that the same thing would happen to him and Claudia as soon as they were living together with her children. "You wait," she'd said. "Pretty soon all *you'll* be talking about is money and the kids' grades. And they won't even be your kids."

She started to cry again, her voice loud, edging toward hysteria. He tried to touch her, but she pulled away and stood panting by herself next to the refrigerator. Suddenly David was in the doorway. He looked at his mother, tears coursing down her face, her hair disheveled. He was sixteen.

"I just thought you ought to know," he said. "You've got the whole second floor wide awake too."

She looked back at him a moment. He was the most beautiful of their children, the most self-contained. He seemed utterly calm in his striped pajamas. Suddenly she wailed and charged at him, her arms flailing. "You! You . . . twerp! You little know-nothing!" She belted him twice, and the sound of flesh smacking flesh was horrible. David turned and covered his head. Alan heard him say, "Don't; don't, Mom," but his own response was slow, too slow, and by the time he rose to protect his son, David had turned again, had opened his arms to embrace his mother, and she covered her face with her hands and let him hold her.

"I'm sorry, Mom," he said. Jody was saying, "Oh, David, oh, David," over and over. David seemed to be crying a little too.

Then Andrea came to the door to see what was happening, and in a fog Alan began to try to explain. Steve's voice shouted down the stairs, "Will someone please tell me what's going on down there?"

Jody and David were still apologizing to each other, laughing breathlessly in relief now. Jody pulled away and got a beer for each of them; and Steve shouted again, "Will somebody just tell me who the survivors are anyhow?"

Andrea went to the foot of the stairs and shouted up, "Mommy and Daddy were having a terrible fight over if he was moving out, and Dave told Mommy she was too noisy, and she hit him. But now it's okay."

"Oh," Steve said. Then he said, "And *is* Dad moving out?"

"I don't know," Andrea called up. She came back to the kitchen doorway. "Are you moving out, Daddy?"

Alan looked at her. He looked at Jody and David. Jody nodded her head.

"Yes," he said.

"You *are?*" Andrea said. "Is he really, Mom?"

"Yes, baby," Jody said.

"Oh, shit," Andrea said, and then she burst into tears. "Why does everything have to happen to me?"

None of Jody's predictions about him and Claudia had come true. If anything, in fact, things had stayed too intense between them. Sometimes an image of Claudia during sex would come to him in the middle of some ordinary task at work and he would feel, embarrassed even if he was by himself, the stirrings of desire. He hadn't been able to relax with his new family. He seemed to be waiting every night for the kids to go to bed so he could be alone with her. He found himself staying later at the clinic than he had to, sometimes missing dinner so he wouldn't have to pass the long evenings pretending to be a father, watching her be a mother. It was, oddly, a repetition of the pattern of turning away that had marked his first marriage, but for entirely different reasons, Alan reminded himself.

During the school year it was better. Her oldest child was in college, and her ex-husband paid for Carol, the middle child, to go to boarding school. Just the youngest, a girl two years younger than Andrea, was at home. But this child, Stephanie, was the one he felt the least comfortable with. He couldn't remember how

Andrea had been two years earlier, but it seemed to him that Stephanie was utterly artificial. Much of her conversation consisted of imitations she did of other people's tones of voice, ways of thinking. They'd drive past someone roller skating and she'd make her voice dopey and say, "Duh, yeah. What I like to do is, unhh, *roll*er skate, yuh. Don't like to read much. Nope. Or talk to much of anyone. Just *wheel* along here." Or in line at a movie, she'd point to a studious-looking kid with glasses and say, "Well, yes, from time to time I like to take in a movie. Of course, it's not as intellectually *stim*ulating as reading philosophy, but even *I* have to relax sometime."

When they passed chain restaurants, she'd do commercials for them verbatim, in a mocking tone. And she quoted her father to Alan constantly. He understood that this was because she was anxious about how she might be betraying him by living with this new father, himself; but he sometimes felt like slapping her when she commented about the way he was doing something by comparing it to the way her father did things.

Alan was a veterinarian. He'd met Claudia when she brought her dog to his office. It was an emergency, and he'd driven in from home to the clinic after the answering service called him. Claudia was parked outside in a big, new-model station wagon. He'd helped her carry the injured dog inside. It had been hit by a car. Claudia stood by the examining table. "Is she going to die?" she asked Alan. She was wearing a pretty flowered sundress smeared with the dog's blood, and she clutched the stained blue bedspread they had used to carry the dog. The animal lay panting, in shock, on the glistening stainless-steel table.

Alan could see that if the dog survived at all, it would be seriously damaged. But he was careful with Claudia, as he usually was with his clients. He felt it was their responsibility to make the final decision, to weigh the pain against what pleasure might remain in life for the animal. "Well, I think we can save her," he'd said. "But it depends on what you want. I mean, there are some people, they have a dog that's maybe blind in one eye, or limps, and they feel like it's nothing, she's fine, she's still getting a lot out of life. But other people feel differently. You just have to decide."

"So she might limp?"

"Minimally, she'll have a limp. We might actually have to amputate in the end. And the eye's gone, that's pretty clear."

Claudia turned away for a moment. Alan watched her throat try to swallow. Her face averted from him, she said, "Well, I think I'd like you to put her down then."

Alan's heart went out to her. "You're sure?" he asked.

Now she nodded firmly. "I guess I'm one of those people who's more concerned, I think, with . . . the quality of life, or something."

Alan lay on his back, watching Claudia undress. She was talking animatedly about their children and how the evening, their first evening all together, had gone. The year before, the two of them had been alone at Christmas. Her children had gone to their father's, and Jody had had his three at home. This year Claudia, who didn't work, had spent weeks preparing for a real family celebration. She had brought to it the same painstaking, passionate energy she invested in everything she did, from sex to cooking. She had even conferred with Jody several times about what presents the kids might need or want.

Now, even though her talk was of the series of inconsequential events that had made up the evening, Alan felt that her gestures, her motions, were all directed at him. He couldn't help thinking for a moment of Jody, her exhausted collapse into bed at the end of the day, often still wearing half the clothes she'd had on all evening. What she did take off, she dropped on the floor around the bed. Coins sometimes rolled noisily out of her pockets to the corners of the room and stayed there weeks, months, before she picked them up. Alan could remember the way they felt when he stepped on them unexpectedly—so cold he'd think for a minute that he'd burned himself on something. In the mornings, all Jody had to do to get dressed was swing her legs out of bed and pull on the jeans she'd left on the floor the night before.

Claudia made a ritual of removing her clothes one item at a time and putting them carefully away. She had delicate underwear and lacy brassieres. Sometimes she wore a garter belt and stockings; and even though they still made love almost every night, she always wore a nightgown when she came to bed. Lifting the hem of the gown, pushing it above her breasts, were gestures which never failed to trigger a sexual response in Alan.

Now she sat at her dressing table, wearing a fragile-looking robe and brushing her hair. With every stroke her breasts bobbled gently. From the living room, where several of their children were still talking, came dim music, a felt bass line rather than a heard melody.

"Marie-France seems sweet, doesn't she?" Claudia was saying.

Marie-France was an exchange student, a friend of Claudia's older daughter, Carol. She was staying through Christmas Day with them. Then she'd go to another friend's house for New Year's. She was grave and pretty. She spoke with a thick French accent, and perhaps also a slight lisp. Twice during the evening she'd excused herself to go out to the front steps to smoke a cigarette. Both times Jeremy, Claudia's son, had gone with her, saying that he needed the air.

Alan had noticed that both of his sons had also sprung to a kind of attention around Marie-France; but in David this was marked by a resolute turning away from her, a lack of focus. Alan had found himself irritated with David because of this. Why couldn't he try harder to get what he wanted, fight for it a little? It was as though he thought he could protect himself from pain by not wanting anything. He ought to have outgrown that idea by now. What was it they said: No pain, no gain?

Alan couldn't remember whether David had been so self-protective before the divorce. But once, shortly afterward, Jody had called him at night, after an evening he'd spent with David. He and Claudia weren't married yet, but her kids were with their father for the night, and he'd called her to come over as soon as he'd returned from dropping David off. When the phone rang, he'd reached for it with hands that smelled of her, and throughout the conversation with Jody the air he breathed was weighted with the scent of Claudia's sex.

"How come you brought David back so early?" Jody had asked.

"We had dinner," he said.

"I thought it was dinner and a movie, or some *time* anyway. Some time alone with each of them each week, you said."

"He didn't seem to want to go to a movie, Jode." He tried to keep his voice from sounding defensive.

"What do you mean, 'didn't seem'?"

"I mean, I read him the list, and about all he said after each one was 'unh huh.' "

Jody was silent a moment. Then she said, "Well, *you* know David." And suddenly Alan was flooded with guilt. As soon as she said it, he did know David. He remembered that David would have needed his sheltering enthusiasm in order to risk wanting to go to a movie. And he'd had it in the back of his mind all evening that if he could just get away early enough, he could be where he was at that moment: in bed with Claudia.

Now Claudia lowered the hairbrush to her lap. "I think Jeremy's madly in love with her," she said.

"With Marie-France?" he asked.

"Yes. Apparently he's been to visit her a couple of times at school. He took her out to dinner once, Carol said. And he was sure pretty obvious about it tonight."

"Steven too," Alan said. But he was thinking of David, who had talked patiently and attentively to Claudia and Stephanie through dinner, and had been awkward whenever Marie-France spoke to him.

"But that's different," Claudia said. "He knows he's too young for her." And then she frowned abruptly. "You know, I'm never going to be able to sleep with that music going. Can you get them to turn it down?"

Alan stiffened slightly. He knew Claudia was speaking of his kids. On their own, Jeremy and Carol rarely used the stereo.

Claudia had given all her children Walkmans several years earlier for just that reason. Sometimes in the evenings when they were home, they would all sit in the living room with their earphones on, in a silence broken only occasionally by their little moans as they hummed along for a second or two.

He got out of bed, put on his robe, and moved noiselessly down the carpeted hall to the top of the stairs. As he passed the open door to Stephanie and Carol's bedroom, he could hear Stephanie doing one of her oddly inflected imitations: "Yes, I just *love* my hair this way, sticking out all over like I've had some electric shock. And I just love pretending it's super-curly when everyone *knows* it's not."

His throat cottoned, and he had to clear it several times at the top of the stairs before he called out, "Dave. David."

His son swung around the corner from the living room, his face lifted, and with the angle up, uncharacteristically open. Alan's heart caught, his voice softened. "Turn it down a bit, would you, son?"

"Sure," David said, and disappeared. The music quieted nearly instantly and Alan could hear Marie-France's thick accent: "But, David, it was just my turn to dance with you."

On the way back to Claudia, Alan stopped at Stephanie's door. She had heard him on the stairs and was turned to face him, her round face whitened with embarrassment.

"And can you girls hold it down in here too?" Alan said loudly. His heart was pounding. "Your mother and I are trying to sleep."

When he got back to the bedroom, Claudia had turned off the light. He put his robe on the chair in the dark and slid into bed next to her. She stayed turned away from him, and Alan knew she had been hurt by his tone in the hall when he spoke to her daughters.

Thursday afternoon, Christmas Eve, it started to snow. Claudia had taken all of her children on a last-minute shopping trip. Through the afternoon the thick flakes fell steadily. By five it seemed to have slowed a little, and Alan asked David to shovel the walk. Andrea went out to help him for a while. Alan was in the kitchen making oyster stew, something he'd always done on Christmas Eve at home, and he could hear Andrea's shrill voice outside as she badgered David. After twenty minutes or so, he heard the front door bang shut, and then she stood in the kitchen, her long hair limp and wet, her cheeks flushed.

"He's no fun, Dad," she said. "Will you come out and have a snowball fight?"

Alan looked at the little pools of water collecting at her feet. "Why isn't he any fun?"

"'Cause whenever Marie-France is around he gets all *serious*. It's boring. He never wants to do anything."

"Marie-France is outside?"

"Yeah. She's helping him shovel."

Alan went into the dark dining room and looked out the window. Against the whited ground, the two figures moved side by side. Marie-France seemed delicate, female in her wool winter coat, like the girls of Alan's youth. Every fourth or fifth shovelful, she and David stood and faced each other for a moment, talking. Their voices were audible only as a murmur, but Marie-France gestured with both hands dramatically when she spoke. Then she'd hook her hair back over her ears and they'd bend to work again; and the distant ringing of the shovels' alternating music would float once more into the warm house.

He went back to the kitchen and told Andrea they could have a snowball fight after dinner.

Claudia and her children came back about six, and the younger girls began setting the table for dinner. Alan and Claudia were sitting in front of the fireplace in the living room with cocktails when Jeremy walked in. Alan offered him some wine or beer, but he refused. He seemed distracted. He sat down and started leafing through a magazine. His mother began to tell him where the wrapping paper was for the presents they'd bought that day. Steve and Carol came in; Steve had challenged her to a game of backgammon before dinner. He was enthusiastic about Alan's offer of a beer. He went to the kitchen and returned with two bottles, one for Carol.

"Glasses too, please, Steven," Claudia said.

"Oh, right," Steve answered cheerfully. And he went out again while Carol set up their game. Alan felt a momentary jealousy at Claudia's ease with his children. He wondered why he couldn't feel that comfortable around hers.

Only a few minutes before Alan was going to get up to serve the stew, the front door opened and Marie-France came in, followed by David.

"Where have *you* been?" Andrea brayed from the dining room. "You're supposed to be helping. It's not fair."

Marie-France laughed and began to take off her coat. "I'm coming immediately," she said.

Jeremy stood and walked closer to the doorway to the hall. "Where were you?" he said quietly to Marie-France.

In spite of himself, Alan felt a moment of pleasure in Jeremy's pinched voice. David. She'd chosen David. Then he was ashamed of this quick pull of his blood. He looked at Claudia, but she was talking to Steve.

Marie-France didn't look at Jeremy. "Don't worry," she said, shaking her coat. "We'll do more than our share. We'll do the dishes, yes, David?"

Alan couldn't see David, who had crossed out of sight to the coat closet; but his voice was light, tense with an unfamiliar joy when he answered. "Whatever Andrea says. She's the absolute boss."

"At least the dishes," Andrea said, standing in the doorway. "Stephanie and me had to do the whole table, *plus* the salad. It's not fair."

Stephanie came and stood next to her. Her hands rose to her hips in imitation of Andrea's posture. "Yeah," she said. "We had to do *everything*."

Alan looked sharply at her, but there seemed to be no contempt, no distance in her echo, and when she and Andrea went back into the dining room, he heard their voices rise and fall animatedly, their mixed laughter.

Alan and Claudia drank a bottle of wine at dinner, and when

Alan began to put on his parka afterward for the snowball fight with Andrea, Claudia came out to the coat closet and said she'd join them, something Jody would never have done. Stephanie and Carol, then Steve, decided it would be fun too; and suddenly the front hall was full of their children, talking loudly to each other, threatening each other cheerfully as they pulled on boots and their puffy nylon coats. Alan, sitting on the stairs to tighten his laces, shut his eyes and listened to them. The whole house seemed to ring with their energy, their goodwill, their togetherness. When he opened his eyes, Claudia stood before him, smiling down at him with deep pleasure, and his heart lifted in gratitude to her.

They poured out of the house onto the front lawn, and began to heave gobs of the wet snow at each other in the glowing light from the downstairs windows. Their footprints crisscrossed the yard as they ran after each other and ducked behind trees and the two parked cars. David and Marie-France came outside when they were finished with the dishes, and finally Jeremy too; and the dark yard echoed with their cries until the falling snow had turned to sleet, then rain, and their mittens and hats were soaked through.

Sometime in the middle of the night, Alan woke abruptly. He heard a noise outside, then a whisper, a cry from downstairs. Claudia muttered in her sleep. She'd been a little drunk when they made love; they'd all had eggnog after the snowball fight, and when they came up to bed, they'd left the four older children and Marie-France still awake, wrapping presents and talking in the living room by the subdued, fragmented light of the Christmas tree.

Alan got up and put on his robe. He shut the bedroom door carefully behind him and walked to the top of the stairs. Just as he started down, he heard a moan in the hall below him. Then Marie-France's voice said, "Oh, stop. Oh, please. Stop."

He hesitated a moment, then continued down. The hall light was off, but he could see Marie-France standing at the front door, by herself. The heavy wooden door was swung in, and she was looking out through the glass storm door. Alan came up behind her. She started and turned to him. Tears stood in her eyes. "Oh, Mr. Griffith, oh, please," she said, and gestured to the door. "They are drunk. We are drunk," she said.

Alan stepped up to the glass. Outside, the night had cleared, and a cold moon rode high above the sloping yard. The snow was silvered with a layer of ice. Sliding across its glistening surface were David and Jeremy in shirtsleeves, each holding the other up, each swinging wildly at the other.

"Oh, please," Marie-France whispered. Her breath smelled rich and sweet, rummy.

But Alan stood frozen, watching the strange silent drama.

David had dropped to one knee now. He held Jeremy around the waist. Jeremy awkwardly hit him several times on the head, while they moved together a few feet down the yard's gentle incline.

David struggled up into Jeremy's embrace. His hands rose to Jeremy's head, held it almost lovingly. Alan watched, unable to move. It wasn't until after David's fist landed on the side of Jeremy's face that he yanked the door open.

They turned to him, startled, drunk, holding each other as though they'd been dancing. Alan stepped outside in his bare feet and the cold slate burned at his soles.

"Get in here," he cried out. "Get in here, you boys."

Then Jeremy let go, and slid away from David. Awkwardly he turned to the house and began to shuffle toward it, as though he were skating. When he opened the storm door behind his stepfather, Alan could hear Marie-France inside, weeping softly.

David was slower, limping. As he passed his father, Alan saw a narrow line of dark blood running from one nostril. He reached out to touch his son, to do something; but David shrugged away from him, as though he were proud of his injury, his pain. "It's fine, Dad," he said. "Don't worry." His voice had the same unfamiliar quality of life and tension Alan had heard in it earlier. "It's nothing," he said, and he moved beyond Alan into the dark hall.